Puffin Books
Bagthorpes v. the World

As usual, life is frantic and funny in the zany Bagthorpe household, but great gloom descends when a bank statement arrives indicating an overdraft of millions. With a fervour born of necessity, Mr Bagthorpe plunges his family into a campaign of self-sufficiency. Soon the garden is full of herbs, vegetables and chickens, all growing rapidly to the sweet strains of Mozart. (Young Tess is a firm believer in the power of good vibrations).

However, it soon becomes clear that all is not well in the garden. Mrs Bagthorpe identifies Tess's lettuce as pansies and snapdragons, while her own flowerbeds bear signs of sprouting beetroot and carrots. Obviously, demon Daisy has been 'helping' again and her good intentions have badly misfired.

Disorder in the garden is second only to the chaos indoors. Grandma Bagthorpe is furtively supplementing the new meagre diet with hampers from Fortnum and Mason, while Great Aunt Lucy announces that she's given up 'time' and insists on eating supper at breakfast and vice versa.

The Bagthorpe Saga (of which this is the fourth book) was made into a very successful television series.

D1494470

Other books by Helen Cresswell

Helen Cresswell

Bagthorpes v. the World

being the fourth part of the
Bagthorpe Saga

Illustrated by Jill Bennett

Puffin Books
in association with Faber and Faber

Puffin Books, Penguin Books Ltd, Harmondsworth, Middlesex, England
Viking Penguin Inc., 40 West 23rd Street, New York, New York 10010, U.S.A.
Penguin Books Australia Ltd, Ringwood, Victoria, Australia
Penguin Books Canada Limited, 2801 John Street, Markham, Ontario, Canada L3R 1B4
Penguin Books (N.Z.) Ltd, 182–190 Wairau Road, Auckland 10, New Zealand

First published in the U.S.A. by Macmillan Publishing Co., Inc. 1979
First published in Great Britain by Faber and Faber 1979
Published in Puffin Books 1982
Reprinted in 1983, 1987

Library of Congress catalog card number 86-43074

Printed and bound in Great Britain by
Cox & Wyman Ltd, Reading
Set in Linotron Bembo

For E. H. Rowe
– without whom The Bagthorpes would never have been.

Chapter One

The Great Bagthorpe Daisy Chain was two weeks old and still the Bagthorpes were not assured of immortality. *The Guinness Book of Records* had been very interested, and had conceded that the Bagthorpes' Chain was the longest yet.

'But the Daisy Season is not yet over,' they wrote, 'and another, longer chain may be recorded before we go to press.'

'Rubbish!' snapped Grandma when she read this. She wrote back saying that if by some freak of nature such a chain were produced, she wished to be notified immediately, so that she could beat *that*, too. As yet no reply had been made to this, and the younger Bagthorpes, at least, were feeling restless and threatened.

'I know we're the *cleverest* family in England,' said Rosie, aged nine, 'but it doesn't necessarily mean we've got the fastest fingers.'

The others gloomily assented that this was so.

'Any fool can string daisies together,' said William, who at sixteen was the eldest, and felt marginally more obliged to prove himself than the rest. 'We should have gone in for a record that takes brains.'

'No one round here thinks we've got brains, any more,' Rosie told him. 'Not after that photo.'

The *Aysham Gazette* had devoted a full half page to a photograph of the Bagthorpes sitting on the front lawn up to their ears in daisies and forking mutton stew into their mouths.

'Zero came out all right in it,' Jack said. 'He was just sitting and acting natural.'

'Which is hardly a picture of the epitome of luminous canine intelligence,' Tess told him.

'Mutton-brained pudding-footed hound,' added William for good measure. (This assessment of Zero's IQ and appearance was in fact Mr Bagthorpe's, but William tended to use it in his absence.)

'If our daisy chain *doesn't* get in *The Guinness Book of Records*, there's not much point in saving it for *my* Records,' said Rosie dolefully. (Keeping Records was one of Rosie's Strings to her Bow.)

No one replied. Enough had already been said about the impractability, not to say downright lunacy, of attempting to preserve for posterity a daisy chain four thousand seven hundred and fifty feet long and consisting of over twenty-two thousand daisies.

'It will be compost within the month,' Mr Bagthorpe told her. 'It will not even be *balanced* compost. Pray do not put it on *my* heap.'

'Archaeologists will be able to piece it together again,' Rosie said obstinately. 'They can piece *anything* together, even things millions of years old. They've got special techniques.'

To this Mr Bagthorpe had returned that even if anyone five hundred years hence did think it worth his while to resurrect a composted daisy chain, the technique required would be of a supernatural, rather than scientific, order.

'It would require a Second Coming,' he declared. 'And do not leave those daisies where I can see them. And stop talking about daisies, the lot of you!'

Mr Bagthorpe was extremely bitter about the Great Bagthorpe Daisy Chain. It had cost him the only chance he had ever had (or was indeed now likely to have) of being seriously interviewed by the *Sunday Times*, and commanding a quarter page in the Review section. Instead, a piece of what Mr Bagthorpe said was unparalleled idiocy had appeared in the Colour Supplement. The only allusion to Mr Bagthorpe and his work had been in parenthesis:

'The Bagthorpe family (the head of which is Henry Bagthorpe, the TV scriptwriter) were discovered by Gerald Pike on the lawn of their home, in pursuit of immortality via a daisy chain . . .'

The accompanying photographs had come out in shaming detail, thanks to Grandma's having had floodlights looped around in branches, on the pretext that threading daisies was trying to her eyes. The only people who liked the photographs and article were Grandma herself, Aunt Celia, and Daisy.

Grandma liked to appear eccentric, and Aunt Celia thought how poetic and symbolic everybody looked, crouched under their dripping umbrellas and knitting daisies. She wrote several poems about it, and encouraged her daughter to do the same. (Daisy, aged five, often wrote poems, especially on walls.)

'If I catch that accursed infant writing any poems on *my* walls,' Mr Bagthorpe warned, 'she will herself be in immediate need of an elegy.' He further said that he would with the utmost pleasure compose one himself.

The Bagthorpes, then, while still unsure of the success of their bid for immortality, threw themselves with increased zeal into their everyday pursuits. They practised frenetically every String to their respective Bows. All the younger Bagthorpes were more or less genii and had several Strings to their Bows, with the exception of Jack, who had none. William (who, his father claimed, had clearly been a tribal warrior in a previous incarnation) beat out long and frenzied tattoos on his new drums. (His old ones had been pierced by Daisy with a knife and fork.) Also, between winning tennis tournaments and attempting to disprove the Theory of Relativity, he held long conversations over his radio with Anonymous, from

Grimsby, a radio pirate with a gift for lugubrious pronouncements and forecasts.

'Anonymous from Grimsby reckons that a UFO came down again last night,' William would announce. Or, 'Anonymous from Grimsby reckons there's an Alien Intelligence in Outer Space. He reckons it's sending out messages in code. He's trying to crack it.'

Nobody but William himself took any of this very seriously, especially Mr Bagthorpe, who would say that even if it were all true, it would still be the least of his problems.

'It's for the Government to worry about,' he would say. 'Let *them* worry. *Any* Alien Intelligence would make less of a mess of things than they do.'

Tess went round the house quoting whole passages in French, mainly from Voltaire, entered a National Judo Contest and spent hours holed up in her room either practising her oboe or endlessly playing Danish Linguaphone records.

Rosie practised the violin, tried to disprove Pythagoras' Theorem, and embarked on a full-scale mural, in oils, of the Great Bagthorpe Daisy-Chain Making.

'That's *bound* to be immortal,' she told everybody. 'Nobody's ever done that before.'

No one commented on this except Mr Bagthorpe, who contented himself with warning her to keep it out of his way. 'If I come across it,' he told her, 'I shall not be accountable for my actions. And stop *talking* about daisies, the lot of you!'

Rosie, despite her father's hostility to the project, was none the less experimenting with different techniques to preserve the daisy chain intact. She tried painting it with colourless nail varnish, glazing it with a starch solution, and squirting it with the stuff used to spray on Christmas trees to keep the needles from falling. The latter worked best, but turned out to be unfeasible. In the first place, it made the chain so stiff that it could not be coiled up, and would have to stay starchly zigzagged all round the garden of Unicorn House for ever. In the second, Rosie worked out that it would cost thirty-nine pounds fourteen pence in Christmas Tree Preserver. She invited the rest of the family to contribute towards this sum, but they declined to a man.

Rosie took a good yardage of the chain to her room and embalmed it, in sections, between pages of the *Junior Encyclopaedia Britannica*, while continuing her experiments to preserve the whole of the chain at a viable economic rate. (If you were a Bagthorpe you never, ever, gave up.)

Mrs Bagthorpe had been little affected one way or another by the daisy chain episode.

'It will be lovely if you all achieve a record,' she told the family, 'and I shall be terribly proud of you. But I do not really believe that this achievement will constitute an extra String to anybody's Bow. I should try to forget the whole matter, for the time being, and concentrate on your *real Strings*' – as, indeed, they were doing.

Mrs Bagthorpe was pleased to note that her offspring had taken this sensible advice, and felt that she had, for once, acted as 'Stella Bright' to her own family. (Mrs Bagthorpe ran a monthly Agony Column in a woman's journal under the name of Stella Bright, but found that as a rule, any advice she might give in her capacity of wife and mother to her own family was rarely taken, let alone effective.)

Mr Bagthorpe tried to work his way through his current problems by battling with a new and unprecedentedly complex script which would, he assured everyone, be 'a breakthrough in the history of television'.

Jack, having no Strings to his Bow, found himself frequently thrown into the sole company of Zero – who belonged to the Bagthorpes in general, and Jack in particular. (He had just turned up in the garden, one day, and

11

stayed.) The Bagthorpes were always running Zero down, and this despite the fact that he was now world-famous, and earned more money than anyone else in the house.

'You and me don't need Strings to our Bows, old chap,' Jack would tell him often. 'Only that lot. And take no notice of what they say. They're just jealous. Good old boy.'

Jack had to do a lot of this kind of praising even now Zero was famous, because he lacked self-confidence and was very easily undermined. When he was, his ears gave him away. They drooped.

Jack tried to bring Zero on during this period while the rest of the family were so obsessively engaged in their various pursuits. He failed, after a period of intensive training, to get Zero to bark up to five, like a dog Jack had once seen in a circus.

'Never mind, old chap,' Jack told him, when he finally gave up. 'It doesn't matter. You don't need to be able to count up to five. I just thought it would be an interest for you. Good old chap.'

Jack was reaching the stage of boredom when he was considering taking out the dowsing rods that had lain in his wardrobe since the Prophet days, and giving them another try, when the letter arrived from the Sainted Aunt.

Letters from Aunt Penelope had been thin on the ground since the Family Reunion débâcle at Easter. Indeed, most of the family had hoped that diplomatic relations would be cut off for a long time to come, if not for ever. Normally, only Mrs Bagthorpe would read her letters (possibly quoting the odd snippet to the rest) and answer them. On this occasion, however, she stopped the whole family in its tracks by reading out the whole thing. The Bagthorpes were all arguing noisily at the time, between mouthfuls of toast or cereal. (Mrs Bagthorpe

12

believed that meals should be civilized occasions, with a brisk and lively interchange of views and opinions, even breakfast.)

'Hush, darlings!' she cried, brandishing the letter. 'You must listen to this!'

Grandma, who had just entered, took her seat, glanced at the missive, and remarked:

'It is from that dreadful woman who married my eldest and best-loved son, and is feeding her family on nuts and grass.'

None of this was true. Henry himself was her favourite son, because he had plenty of fight, and she could conduct frequent and truly stupendous rows with him. Aunt Penelope and Uncle Claud had certainly turned vegetarian but did not, so far as the others knew, eat grass. No one, however, argued. It was a whole lot of trouble to argue with Grandma, and on this occasion, definitely not worth it.

'Luke has already reached the semi-final of the Young Brain of Britain Contest,' Mrs Bagthorpe exclaimed, ignoring this interruption.

This intelligence met with stony silence from her offspring and a further speech from Grandma.

'She will never rear those children,' she said. 'If, indeed, they *are* children. Why do they never raise their voices? Why do they never shout? Their blood has been turned to water.'

'Their brains haven't,' said Rosie gloomily. 'Trust that revolting Luke. I bet he cheated.'

'Let me read you the whole letter,' said Mrs Bagthorpe. 'It is full of news.'

Mr Bagthorpe looked up from behind his newspaper.

'I shall not be required to listen, I hope,' he said. 'I am engaged in an extremely complex and demanding creative exercise, and the least thing will destroy my balance. If necessary, I shall cover my ears.'

He retreated behind his paper, and Mrs Bagthorpe took a deep breath and prepared to regale her unenthusiastic audience.

'"Dear Laura",' she read. '"We trust and pray that yourself, dear Henry, and the family are thriving and well, despite your corrupt diet".'

There came here a snort from behind Mr Bagthorpe's newspaper which seemed to indicate that he was not managing not to listen.

'"There is very little news to tell",' Mrs Bagthorpe continued, '"other than that Claud and myself feel so blessed in our children, and are continually offering up thanks for them. I am sending under separate cover an inscribed copy of the volume in which four of dear little Esther's poems appear. And I know that you will all be thrilled to hear that dear Luke has now reached the semi-final of the radio Young Brain of Britain Contest. He is, indeed, the youngest child ever to do so".'

William muttered something under his breath and to Jack it sounded like 'Bloody *hell!*' It may have sounded like this to his mother, as well, because she frowned reprovingly over the top of the letter before continuing.

'"Claud and I are naturally exceedingly proud of them both, and I know that you will rejoice with us. 'And Solomon's wisdom exceeded the wisdom of all the children of the east country and all the wisdom of Egypt.' (I Kings, Chapter 4, verse 30.) You will be interested to know that tomorrow dear Great Aunt Lucy is coming to be our guest for several days".'

'What?' Here Mr Bagthorpe threw down his newspaper on the marmalade pot and abandoned all pretence of not listening.

'"We have always been so fond of her,"' continued his wife, '"and the dear children write to her almost every week. We shall do all possible to make her stay happy, and also to see the error of her ways and turn to a more natural and wholesome diet. Blessings on you all. God be with you. Penelope."'

'Hell's bells!' fumed Mr Bagthorpe. 'The woman's a – she's a whited sepulchre. A snake in the grass. She's a worm in the –'

'That is enough, Henry,' said Grandma, interrupting her son's flow of mixed metaphors. 'We all know perfectly well why you are in this childish tantrum. You do not deceive us for a moment. You care not a fig for Lucy.'

This was true. Mr Bagthorpe did, at rare intervals, make a fleeting visit to Great Aunt Lucy (a distant connection on his father's side), in Torquay. He did this partly to get away from his own family, and partly because Great Aunt Lucy had few surviving relatives and was extremely rich. The thought that Aunt Penelope was now also putting herself in the way of a hefty bequest was too much for him.

'She will be driven mad within the week by that bunch of Latter Day Saints!' Mr Bagthorpe fulminated, 'and as likely as not alter her will while the balance of her mind is disturbed by nuts and water.' He then rounded on his own offspring. 'Why don't you lot write letters every week?' he demanded. 'What's the matter with you? Have you *no* concept of which side your bread is buttered?'

'I don't think I ever really do anything Great Aunt Lucy would be interested in,' said Jack honestly. His siblings were all more concerned with Luke than the matter of bequests, and suchlike.

'She'll have to come here,' Mr Bagthorpe said. 'Invite her, Laura. Do it now.'

'But, Henry, darling, you are in the middle of such a difficult piece of work,' his wife protested.

'To hell with that,' he said tersely. 'Invite her. And you lot – you just keep yourselves within bounds while she's here. I warn you. I can hardly afford to keep you as it is.

If I am now to be sold down the river for a mess of pottage, I shall certainly not be able to afford it.'

'You could always borrow off Zero,' suggested Jack helpfully. 'He'd lend you some, wouldn't you, old chap?'

Zero made a movement of his tail that could in no way be described as enthusiastic, and Mr Bagthorpe pushed back his chair and stood up.

'*That* piece of uncalled-for sarcasm is all I needed,' he said. 'The day I am reduced to borrowing money from a dog – and in particular a numskulled, pudding-footed, matted-up hound like –'

'Don't, Father!' pleaded Jack. 'I'm sorry. I didn't meant it like that. I didn't mean to be sarcastic.'

Jack did not even know how to be sarcastic. He often wished he did, so that he could keep his end up with the rest of the family. And he could see that Zero already seemed to be lying closer to the ground under Mr Bagthorpe's onslaught, his nose buried under his paws, his ears wilting.

Mr Bagthorpe flung out. He was muttering under his breath, but Jack could hear only the odd words, like 'bankruptcy' and 'last ditch' and 'penury'.

'What a pity Henry is so impulsive and so bad-tempered,' remarked Grandma, spooning up honey. 'He should have taken up the offer of a loan from the dog, which I should imagine would almost certainly have been interest-free. It was extremely clever of you, Jack, to think of such a thing, and I hope that if the contingency arises, the same offer will be made to myself.'

'Of course, Grandma,' Jack told her, warmed by the unaccustomed compliment. Like Zero, he hardly ever got praised.

'I'm off,' announced William bitterly, pushing back his own chair. 'I hope they all die of food poisoning.'

Everyone knew whom he meant.

'William, dear!' murmured his mother in shocked

tones as the door slammed. 'Oh dear, perhaps I should not have read out the letter at all.'

A blight had certainly been cast over the entire household except Grandma, who scented trouble in large doses ahead, and had perked up considerably as the row had developed. Grandpa, who was almost deaf and probably had his hearing aid switched off, beamed round at everyone and observed:

'Warmer, today. Not far off the wasp season.' He folded his napkin and rose.

As he made his exit the knob of the outer door to the kitchen turned, and Mrs Fosdyke entered. (She came in daily to do for the Bagthorpes, but refused to live in.)

'Morning,' she said, whipping off her headscarf and coat. 'I'm late on account of the marge, you'll remember, Mrs Bagthorpe?'

'Marge?' repeated Mrs Bagthorpe, her mind elsewhere.

'What you asked for from the shop.' Mrs Fosdyke slapped down four packets of this commodity. 'And the shop not open till half eight, as you'll remember.'

'No — yes — of course. Thank you so much, Mrs Fosdyke.'

'You have some good news to impart to Mrs Fosdyke have you not, Laura?' said Grandma, seizing the chance to stir troubled waters. Mrs Fosdyke had by now exchanged her shoes for the fur-edged slippers she wore winter and summer alike to 'keep off the cramps', and was noisily rattling dishes in the sink. Mrs Fosdyke's tendency to equate noisiness with efficiency was one of her less endearing traits, and one that frequently drove Mr Bagthorpe to near-breaking point.

'Oh. Yes. Well.' Mrs Bagthorpe seemed nervous. 'I wonder, Mrs Fosdyke, if you are in a position to cater for a house guest some time in the near future? Only one person, and I should think very little trouble.'

At this Mrs Fosdyke turned and wiped her hands on her flowered overall.

'Not one of them vegitinarians, I hope?' she inquired suspiciously. 'I can't say I'm up to that, not at the minute. My nerves still ain't up to what they were.'

Mrs Fosdyke's nerves had been badly affected during the Family Reunion. She had been forced to grate endless carrots and apples for the Latter Day Saints, and had been showered with maggots on two separate occasions.

'The lady concerned is an elderly relation of Mr Bagthorpe's,' Mrs Bagthorpe now assured her, 'and I should think would find raw foods quite indigestible. I should imagine that a light, bland diet would be more suitable, with plenty of junkets and custards and –'

'Relative of Mr Bagthorpe's?' Mrs Fosdyke interrupted. 'Never that old woman from Torquay!'

'Great Aunt Lucy certainly does live in Torquay, Mrs Fosdyke,' said Mrs Bagthorpe rather coolly.

'Never her that's got that Pekingese and that parrot that's always fighting? There'll be no Pekingese and parrots, I hope?'

'Whether or not Wung Foo is still living I am not certain,' replied Mrs Bagthorpe, 'but the parrot is definitely dead.'

'Got killed, did it?' asked Mrs Fosdyke. 'By that dog?'

'I believe it did,' Mrs Bagthorpe told her. 'So I hope that will put your mind at rest, Mrs Fosdyke.'

The latter sniffed and turned back to the sink. During the past year, while so many family meals were taken in the kitchen because of the burned-out and unusable dining- and sitting-rooms, Mrs Fosdyke had heard more than the usual number of Bagthorpian rows and arguments. Her mind was by no means put at rest. As she swished the suds into the water she tried to remember some of the things Mr Bagthorpe had said about his Aunt Lucy after his last brief visit. She could not at the moment recall details, but definitely remembered that they had been unflattering, and had given herself, Mrs Fosdyke, the distinct impression that Great Aunt Lucy was at least as mad as the rest of the Bagthorpes and possibly madder.

By the time she *had* remembered the missing details, it would be too late either to stop Great Aunt Lucy coming or for Mrs Fosdyke to hand in her notice. The die would have been cast, and events plummeting out of the control of herself or anybody else. Another blood-freezing chapter in the Bagthorpe Saga had begun.

Chapter Two

Within twenty-four hours of the arrival of the letter from the Sainted Aunt, the whole household was disorientated to a degree hardly ever before known. Everybody's feelings were divided. One and all of them could see that it would be a good thing if Great Aunt Lucy left most of her money to themselves, rather than to the hateful Dog-collar Brigade. Nobody, on the other hand, wished to entertain this relative. They had all heard the odd remark made about her by Mr Bagthorpe, and even making due allowance for his tendency to gross exaggeration, nobody much liked the sound of the old lady.

Mr Bagthorpe himself went unusually quiet, and kept to his study for most of the day. He did this because he did not wish to be cross-examined about Great Aunt Lucy, as he certainly would have been had he emerged. It was then possible that the invitation would be withdrawn. Mr Bagthorpe had told his family a few things about her, but by no means all. He alone was aware, for instance, that Great Aunt Lucy did not have Strings to her Bow, she had what in his experience was far more deadly – Bees in her Bonnet.

Each time Mr Bagthorpe visited her the old lady had done a complete turnabout in her view on practically everything, and he had in fact told the family that no one else he knew could change their stance on any given subject with such inconsequence and speed.

'Her mind revolves like a spinning top,' he had said. 'She can turn through three hundred and sixty degrees in ten minutes flat.'

He said that many politicians had this ability, and indeed needed it, but it was extremely unsettling to live with. This was why his visits to Torquay had rarely lasted longer than two days. And it was certainly why he had been so shaken by the intelligence that she was to visit the Dogcollar Brigade. She was, he well knew, perfectly capable of being converted to vegetarianism within an hour of arrival. And if she were, there would, he also knew, be no half measures.

'She will probably even try to make that accursed Peke of hers eat grass,' he thought glumly, 'and will certainly require all of us to.'

He mentally resolved to look up a few books on nutrition during the days prior to Aunt Lucy's visit, so that he could put forward a sufficiently powerful argument in favour of a meat diet to send her weathercock of a mind round through one hundred and eighty degrees.

'In which case,' he thought fatalistically, 'she will probably wish to roast an ox whole on the front lawn, or have us all eating raw hedgehogs.'

Fortunately, Grandma was not aware of the full extent of Great Aunt Lucy's eccentricity. Had she been, she would certainly have managed to put some kind of a spoke in the wheel to prevent her coming. She had, as it was, misgivings, but at present she kept these to herself. She had met this relative only once, many years ago, at a wedding, and remembered that she had worn the largest hat and more jewellery than anyone else present. Grandma accordingly did a good deal of rummaging through her own drawers for articles of adornment that would ensure her keeping her own end up in this respect.

The visitor was incontrovertibly *older* than Grandma (she was eighty-seven – older than Grandpa, even) and this in itself seemed to threaten her own position. The Bagthorpes deferred a lot to Grandma because of her age and she did not wish to appear relatively less august in their eyes. She was also aware that the other old lady had claims to oddness, though she did not yet know about the Bees in the Bonnet. Grandma comforted herself with the thought that she was on home ground, and had years of experience in manipulating the Bagthorpes, and that if it came to a showdown, she would probably win. The prospect of a showdown on a large scale in itself appealed strongly to Grandma.

The younger Bagthorpes had never met their Great Aunt before and were not looking forward to their roles as sycophants. They were even less used than the average person to flattering and pleasing other people. They boasted a lot, but tended to ignore, or even decry, the achievements of others. Luke's meteoric rise towards becoming Young Brain of Britain was making them all feel threatened. William, indeed, was spending a lot of time up in his room on the top floor fiddling with his radio equipment, in the hope that he might find a way of sabotaging the programme when it went out.

'If I can jam it,' he told the others, 'I definitely shall. The B B C can take whatever action they like.'

Tess suggested that if by the date the radio programme went out William was still not able to jam it, they might try another method of bringing about Luke's downfall. She had been reading lately a good many books about ESP, and wanted the Bagthorpes to try blanketing Luke with thought waves. She said that if they all sat round in a circle holding hands and with their eyes shut, every time Luke was asked a question they could instantly send out powerful telepathic thoughts of the wrong answer.

'We all have powerful brains, except Jack,' she told them, 'and our combined thought waves will be exceedingly strong.'

This suggestion aroused extremely hostile reactions from the others, who wanted no part, they said, in anything so silly. In the end, however, after Tess had quoted some convincing instances from books by Jung and

Arthur Koestler, they reluctantly agreed that they would, as a last resort, try this.

'Though we shall have to lock the door first,' William said. 'None of us will be able to hold up our heads again if we're caught at it.'

The entire Bagthorpe household was, then, under threat of some kind or other, and none more so than Mr Bagthorpe himself. It needed only the slightest nudge, he felt, to topple the balance of his mind and send it plummeting into full-scale schizophrenia or paranoia.

This nudge, which could hardly be described as slight, came the following day, when his current bank statement arrived. Everybody saw the nudge, because it happened at breakfast. Rosie dropped his mail on to his plate and he snatched it up instantly, as he always did, to see if any cheques had arrived from the BBC. He sorted deftly through the pile, putting anything in a buff envelope into a separate pile. Mr Bagthorpe had the profoundest suspicion of anything in a buff envelope, and had once missed claiming a handsome prize in a sweepstake because he had left the communication relating to this lying with a pile of unopened bills for over three months.

Today, nothing in the *white* envelopes seemed to be giving Mr Bagthorpe much pleasure, and there was certainly no cheque from the B B C.

'Why the devil do they not pay me?' he demanded of the company at large, flinging his white correspondence aside. 'I am constantly meeting *their* deadlines, why cannot they meet mine? I shall almost certainly have to go on strike.'

He frequently threatened this kind of industrial action, but never carried it out, because he was afraid that in the absence of himself another scriptwriter would step into his shoes, probably permanently.

'What's this?' His eye fell on the top buff envelope. 'Bank statement!'

23

He was well into his stride now and, knowing that the contents would provide him with further ammunition, took the unprecedented action of opening the envelope there and then. He picked up his marmalade-smeared knife and slit the top. The Bagthorpes watched, because they knew he would almost certainly be overdrawn, and would accordingly put on a full-scale performance. They were, however, by no means prepared for the reactions that followed.

The first thing that happened was that Mr Bagthorpe went perfectly white. Then his mouth opened soundlessly. Then his face flushed dark red. His eyes were glazed. Then he went white again and his mouth worked, but still no sound was emitted. The younger Bagthorpes were more fascinated than concerned by this performance, but Mrs Bagthorpe was moved to inquire sympathetically:

'Not bad news, I hope, darling?'

Mr Bagthorpe looked up at this, and his voice now came out with such force that everyone present jumped and Mrs Fosdyke dropped a saucer in the sink.

'Bad news?' he yelled. 'Bad news? Oh my God!'

'What? What is it?' Mrs Bagthorpe, though no stranger to her husband's histrionics, was alarmed.

'We're bankrupted! It's happened! I knew it would, I knew it would!' He was gabbling now, and clutching at his hair with the free hand that was not brandishing the bank statement. 'Those infernal bureaucrats have smashed me! They've been after me for years, and now they've got me!'

He seemed well into a full-scale paranoia.

'Calm yourself, Henry!' said Mrs Bagthorpe helplessly. She rose and went down the table. 'Let me see.'

She stretched out a hand, but he snatched the paper back.

'All those noughts!' he gibbered. 'Hundreds, thousands – oh my God – millions! I haven't counted them. I daren't! I daren't!'

'Has he *really* gone mad, d'you think?' Rosie whispered to Jack. 'He often nearly does. Has he really, d'you think?'

Mr Bagthorpe began to laugh jerkily and spasmodically, as if sneezing.

'Might've,' Jack whispered back.

'Now, Henry.' Mrs Bagthorpe was being firm and sensible now, being Stella Bright. 'Give that to me.'

Mr Bagthorpe had the bank statement crushed against his chest. Now he slowly drew it out and held it at arm's length. Quickly his eyes flickered over it.

'It is, it is! It's true! Rows of noughts!'

Mrs Bagthorpe took advantage of his renewed gibbering to snatch the statement away. The young Bagthorpes watched as she straightened it out.

'Oh!' she gasped.

'You see! You see!' almost shrieked Mr Bagthorpe. 'They've got me! They've been out to get me for years!'

His audience knew, by and large, whom he meant by 'they'. He meant the Tax Inspector, the Customs and Excise, the GPO, the Local Council, the Electricity Board and now, it appeared, his own bank.

'It is a mistake,' said Mrs Bagthorpe firmly. 'Quite clearly. Do pull yourself together, Henry. No one can possibly be overdrawn by a figure containing that number of noughts.'

'How much is it?' inquired William, who was one of the family's walking computers – the other being Rosie.

'It's – it's – I don't know,' admitted Mrs Bagthorpe. 'I have never seen so many noughts.'

'There you are! I told you! I told you!' Mr Bagthorpe gibbered. 'I can't pay it, I can't! If I wrote a script a day for the next twenty years, I still couldn't! It's jail – I shall be put in jail!'

Mrs Fosdyke, later describing the scene to her cronies in the Fiddler's Arms, was inclined to agree with Mr Bagthorpe about this.

'The wonder is he wasn't put in jail years ago,' she told them. 'He's not right in the head. If I was Mrs Bagthorpe I should leave him, I should, and let him play his noughts and crosses by himself. That dog of theirs has got more sense than he has.'

'Henry, somewhere, somehow, a computer has gone wrong,' said Mrs Bagthorpe loudly and distinctly.

This served only to heighten his hysteria.

'Computer!' he shrieked. 'I knew it! I knew it!'

Mr Bagthorpe had this theory that the country was run not by politicians, as people supposed, but by computers. The politicians, he said, were only front men, the pawns of the computers, which explained why they were all so stupid. Grandma sometimes argued about this, when she felt like it, and would ask him who, in that case, was working the computers? To this he would reply that nobody did, because the computers themselves had now taken on a life of their own, and become autonomous.

'The last real politician this country had was Aneurin

Bevan,' he would maintain. 'You are wasting your time arguing with me. I am convinced of it.'

There certainly seemed little use in arguing with him on this occasion, and the only person likely to do so was Grandma, who entered at this juncture, having heard her son's agonized bellowings from her room. She had not wasted time dressing for fear of missing a good scene, and her hair was uncombed.

'Good morning,' she greeted the family.

'Oh Mother, are you not well?' asked Mrs Bagthorpe anxiously.

'I am perfectly well, thank you, Laura,' she replied, 'and hope that you are all the same.'

Mr Bagthorpe groaned.

'Are *you* not well, Henry?' inquired his mother.

'Why cannot people opt out of society?' said Mr Bagthorpe, ignoring the question. 'I want to opt out.'

'I have no idea why you should wish to take such a step,' Grandma told him, 'and can only suppose you have read something in the paper that has upset you again. You should take no notice of the papers. As I have frequently told you, they are a tissue of lies. You yourself should know that words can be manipulated to mean anything at all.'

Mr Bagthorpe was in no mood for a lecture from Grandma about the perniciousness of the word, either written or spoken. He had heard it all before. She had a very carefully prepared and rehearsed speech on the subject which she trotted out whenever she saw the opportunity, to detract from the worth of his own calling.

'Any words you have to say to me are wasted, Mother,' he interrupted. 'I am not in my right mind. I think I am now schizophrenic.'

'Henry has had a rather upsetting bank statement,' Mrs Bagthorpe explained.

'Upsetting?' Mr Bagthorpe threatened to take right off again. 'Upsetting?'

'Henry, of course, is very easily upset,' observed Grandma. 'Might I have a coffee, Mrs Fosdyke, please? By how much are you overdrawn this time, Henry?'

'A few billion, at a rough guess,' William told her. 'Can *I* see the statement, Mother?'

'And me,' piped up Rosie. 'I'll work it out for you, Father.'

'Certainly not,' Mrs Bagthorpe said. 'I think we should now let the whole matter drop.'

'Whole matter drop,' repeated Mr Bagthorpe in hollow tones. 'I shall be in a debtor's prison for the remainder of my life, like that chap in *Little Dorrit*. And it's my luck that I can't make sure that you lot have to as well. No one is going to convince me that an overdraft that size was achieved single-handed. It resembles the National Debt. I am a man of moderate tastes and live most abstemiously. It is the wanton and reckless squandering of money by my dependants that –'

'That really will do Henry,' Mrs Bagthorpe was now moderately cross, despite having determinedly taken several very deep breaths during the course of the incident. 'You had better go and telephone your bank manager immediately and ascertain the true extent of your overdraft. You are now being silly.'

'I have never been overdrawn in my entire life,' said Grandma piously. 'I was brought up to consider any sort of debt disgraceful.'

'And who brought *me* up?' demanded Mr Bagthorpe triumphantly.

'I freely admit that I made a failure of your upbringing,' she returned calmly. 'We are none of us perfect, even myself. I did as well with you as any mother possibly could. That I failed is one of my greatest sorrows, and I think it most insensitive, Henry, to throw it at me in this way.'

'You made a fair old mess of Celia, if it comes to that,' continued her son remorselessly. 'Spouting poetry, throwing clay, nibbling lettuces. And look what *she* produced by way of progeny.'

He was referring to Daisy Parker, Aunt Celia's five-year-old daughter. It was unusual for him to refer to her, because by and large he tried to pretend that she did not exist. He only did so now because a powerful friendship had recently sprung up between Daisy and Grandma. They were known within the family as The Unholy Alliance. (There was sometimes a third party to this, known as Arry Awk, invisible to the ordinary human eye, but apparently well known and loved by Daisy.)

'Daisy is a shining jewel of a child,' said Grandma, predictably rising to the defence of her favourite. 'The fact that she is flesh of my flesh and blood of my blood is a constant source of pride and joy to me. She is the solace of my old age. I am glad that you have reminded me of her, Henry. I shall telephone The Knoll directly after breakfast, and see whether Celia will allow her to come and stay for a few days.'

'That,' said Mr Bagthorpe, 'is all I need. In that case, I shall go and stay with Aunt L –'

He broke off sharply. Aunt Lucy was not in Torquay. She was staying with the Latter Day Saints. Mr Bagthorpe was desperate, but not sufficiently desperate to consider a visit to them. His unfeeling offspring, seeing his discomfiture, tittered.

Mr Bagthorpe stood up.

'I am a broken man,' he declared. He tossed down the crumpled bank statement, which was instantly seized upon by William and Rosie, and tore loudly in half. '*You* ring the bank, Laura,' he told his wife. 'You can then break the news gently to me later. I must go to my study and revise my entire philosophy of life. The kind of trauma I have suffered lately has left me a changed man.'

He went out to revise his world view, and left his family to sort out his finances.

Chapter Three

Mr Bagthorpe's bank overdraft turned out to be only in three figures, as usual. He was not comforted by this.

'The damage has already been done,' he asserted. 'I have suffered an irreversible trauma, and shall never be the same again. I am either schizophrenic, or paranoiac, or both. I am not certain. I shall have to consult my Laing. In either case, the roots of my malady certainly lie within the family itself.'

At first the family did not believe this, but when the widening rings of his schizophrenia began to impinge on their own lives, they were forced to take more serious note of his claim. There could be little doubt that Mr Bagthorpe, for whatever reasons, was now in the grip of a fully developed, all-out obsession.

The form this obsession took was what Tess described as a 'Scrooge Complex'.

'He has focused all his subconscious anxieties on to one,' she told the others. 'He has tried to simplify his personal neuroses by converting them into something with which he feels he can cope – money.'

'But Father *can't* cope with money,' Rosie pointed out. 'You know he can't.'

'But his anxieties have at least been *externalized*,' Tess explained.

Nobody had the least idea what she was talking about.

'If you read much more Jung and Laing, you will go the same way yourself,' William told her. 'I think that you have more inherited genes from Father than any of us. That is a poor look out.'

Mr Bagthorpe astounded everyone by telling Mrs Fosdyke, just before lunch, that she could go home.

'Take the afternoon off,' he told her.

'But I ain't poorly,' Mrs Fosdyke objected. 'And what about the washing up? And what about the blancmange for tea?'

'We shall deal with the washing up and the blancmange,' he told her.

She was clearly stumped. Nothing like this had ever happened before. Knowing Mr Bagthorpe as she did, Mrs Fosdyke viewed this gesture of apparent magnanimity with the darkest suspicion.

'He's up to something,' she told Mesdames Pye and Bates later over her Guinness. 'You mark my words. There's more in this than meets the eye.'

'Could be that he's unhinged by being bankrupted,' suggested Mrs Pye with relish. 'You did say he was bankrupted, didn't you, Glad?'

'Oh, definite,' Mrs Fosdyke assured her.

She went on to say that she believed Mr Bagthorpe was trying to ease her gradually into redundancy.

'Which you ain't allowed to do,' she said. 'Not these days. And even if you do, you've got to give a Silver Handshake.'

Mrs Fosdyke was not far off the truth in her prognosis, except that Mr Bagthorpe was not intending to give her a Golden, Silver, or any other kind of Handshake on her departure – not even one of the ordinary variety, if he could avoid it. He had never made any secret of his dislike of Mrs Fosdyke, and if any cuts were to be made, then clearly her services must be dispensed with as soon as possible.

'We can no longer afford Mrs Fosdyke,' he told them all, after her departure in what seemed to them unreasonable dudgeon. 'She is a luxury. Not only do we have to pay her wages, but she is day after day wearing out my carpets with her perpetual hedgehogging about with the hoover, and moreover has inflated ideas about what kind of meals we can afford. We cannot afford beef. We cannot afford rich pastry and pork pies. Tess, you will kindly make the blancmange for tea. And use half milk and half water.'

'But I don't know how,' Tess protested.

'Then learn,' he told her tersely. 'Read the instructions on the packet. We are now beginning to find the chinks through which the winds of the world howl!'

No one could make anything of this latter obscure utterance, other than it did seem to indicate that Mr Bagthorpe's mind had indeed become, at least temporarily, deranged.

Mrs Bagthorpe tried to humour her husband by agreeing that their diet was perhaps too rich, and that in the interests of both health and economy, it should possibly be simplified.

'But as to dispensing with the services of Mrs Fosdyke,' she said. 'I really cannot agree. You will remember, Henry, how disrupted the household became in her absence earlier this summer.'

'This household *is* going to be disrupted,' he told her. 'The four horsemen of the Apocalypse are going to drive a coach and pair right through it. And Mrs Fosdyke will be trampled down in the process.'

'I have not the least idea what you are talking about, Henry,' said his wife, becoming tight-lipped. 'If necessary, I shall pay for Mrs Fosdyke's services out of my own money. I, too, am a breadwinner, and must be allowed some say in the management of things.'

'You do as you like,' he told her, 'but I warn you – I shall cut off the electricity at the mains at eight o'clock each morning.'

An electrified silence followed this stark pronouncement.

'I do not think I quite heard you, Henry,' said his wife at length.

'I think you did,' he returned. 'There will be nothing to prevent people filling flasks with hot drinks if they feel that they cannot get through the day without them. And there are, of course, methods of cooking which require nothing more than a bag of straw or a sandpit, or something. We shall use these methods in future.'

At some time Mr Bagthorpe had evidently read articles on self-sufficiency, and was now drawing on confused memories of these.

'We could always have salad every day,' suggested William with an attempt at sarcasm, 'like the Sainted Aunt.'

'There is no way this family will eat salads, with tomatoes at the price they are,' said Mr Bagthorpe stringently. 'When we have grown our own salad stuff, then we shall eat it.'

'Oh *dear*!' Mrs Bagthorpe felt quite helpless.

'I already have a row of cos lettuce,' he continued, 'and one of spring onions. There is also, I believe, some beetroot and rhubarb. We shall have to exercise our ingenuity with these ingredients.'

The Bagthorpes sat and bleakly pondered the prospect of such a diet.

'Go and fetch your grandmother, dear,' said Mrs Bagthorpe to Rosie, sotto voce. Mr Bagthorpe heard.

'There is nothing Mother can do,' he told his wife. 'This is my household. If she prefers to go and live with Claud or Celia, then that is her affair. If she went to Celia's, she could live on caviare and gin.'

Grandma, when the situation had been outlined to her, did not in fact opt for either of these alternatives. She scented a good deal of excitement and conflict ahead.

'I shall simply have a hamper sent from Fortnum and Mason each week,' she announced. 'Will you commence this absurd policy before the visit of Lucy, or after?'

'We shall commence it forthwith,' he said. 'If there is one thing that can be said for Aunt Lucy, it is that she admires determination and strength of character. She will observe a good deal of both these qualities during her stay.'

'But what about being *immortal*?' Rosie wailed. 'What about getting famous before that horrible Luke does? If we're all washing pots and digging and sowing seeds how can we do our Strings to our Bows?'

'That is enough of that kind of talk,' her father told her sternly. 'What this family is now concerned with is Survival. The whole world is ranged up out there against us. We shall shore up our defences against it. We shall become, in fact, totally Self-Sufficient. Only when we have achieved that shall we become free.'

'But, Henry, I feel free already!' cried Mrs Bagthorpe desperately. 'Why do you not take the afternoon off and go for a nice long walk?'

'Because I never go for long walks,' he replied, 'as you know full well, Laura. I detest long walks. I shall spend the afternoon tilling the soil. And then, this evening I shall draw up a rota of duties for the whole household.'

'Pray do not put me down for anything,' Grandma requested. 'I am too old to be caught up in this sort of hocus pocus. Wisdom, I am happy to say, comes with age.'

'Bilge, Mother,' Mr Bagthorpe told her. 'You have never been wise, nor are you now. Age has simply compounded your unreason. The day you get to be wise, will be the day cows fly. And we shall, of course, have to get one.'

'Why will we?' demanded Tess.

'Because,' he told her, 'we shall require milk. Milk is necessary for bones and teeth and so forth. We can have a cow, or we can have a goat. You can take your pick.'

'Who'll milk it?' Jack asked.

'You, probably,' replied Mr Bagthorpe. 'The time has come when you are going to have to pay the way of that mutton-headed hound of yours. What does he cost to feed? What contribution does he make to this benighted household? There is no room for drones in this hive.'

There was nothing much that Jack could say in reply to this, because Zero did not in fact do much about the house, not even frighten off burglars.

'He makes money,' Jack said stoutly, 'and he doesn't cost you anything, Father. He gets free Buried Bones, remember. Anyway, I don't mind milking a goat as long as somebody shows me how to do it.'

'And who will that be?' inquired Tess. 'Can *you* milk a goat, Father?'

'There is no doubt a perfectly good manual on the subject,' he told her, unperturbed, 'which is more than Robinson Crusoe had the benefit of. Where is your spirit of adventure?'

The spirit of adventure seemed at a very low ebb throughout the household. The only person who appeared to have it to any marked degree was Mr Bagthorpe himself, who, being now gripped by the notion of Survival, was fast spiralling out of control.

'The summer house will be converted to a chicken house,' he informed everybody, the idea having just occurred to him. 'We shall thus have the benefit of free range eggs.'

'But if the hens are roaming about free, they'll eat all the lettuce and salads,' objected Rosie.

'Do not bother me with irksome details,' Mr Bagthorpe told her. 'I am concerned with evolving a Master Plan for Survival. It will be up to you lot to see to the details. I read an article recently about how to generate electricity from sewage and dung. You, William, had better

look into it. At last your expensive and heretofore point-
less interest in electricity will pay off.'

'It's not electricity, it's electronics,' William protested.
'They're two separate things.'

Mr Bagthorpe could not be brought to see this. A man
who will not carry a computer, despite his lack of arith-
metic, because he insists that it is giving off dangerous
radioactive rays inside his pocket, is unlikely to appreciate
any fine shades of meaning in the scientific field.

'Electricity – electronics – what's the difference?' he said.
'I am disappointed in the way you are all reacting. There
will be no malingering. It is also possible to generate electricity from a windmill, and you had better look into that
as well. We cannot afford to waste anything, even the
wind.'

There now fell a silence – a rare occurrence at a Bagthorpe meal. Everyone present – with the exception of
Grandma and Mr Bagthorpe himself – was now thoroughly frightened. It was becoming clearer by the minute
that Mr Bagthorpe was in deadly earnest. There was not
even any point in sending for Dr Winters. He had made it
clear enough in the past that he considered Mr Bagthorpe
mad, and that he was not interested in treating this condi-
tion. He probably thought it untreatable.

The silence was eventually broken by the sound of
spurting gravel from the other side of the house. Mrs
Bagthorpe instantly leapt up and hurried to greet the visitors.

'Russell – Celia – thank heaven you are here!' Jack
heard her say. 'Do come and see if you can do anything
with Henry!'

'He has not, I hope, been standing on his head again?'
came Uncle Parker's voice.

'I can hear you!' yelled Mr Bagthorpe. 'Come on in
here! It's no good hatching things up out there!'

Mrs Bagthorpe re-entered, followed by Uncle Parker,

Aunt Celia and Daisy, the latter almost totally eclipsed by a large, beribboned parcel.

'Hallo, all!' Uncle Parker greeted them affably. 'Hallo, Grandma. Daisy's got something for you.'

Daisy advanced and plonked her parcel in front of Grandma, dislodging a plate as she did so. It fell to the floor and shattered.

'Oh *dear!*' squealed Daisy.

'You will pay for that, Russell,' said Mr Bagthorpe. 'We can no longer afford to underwrite your daughter's destructive behaviour. Does she go *anywhere* without wreaking havoc?'

'Hush, Henry!' cried Aunt Celia. 'Daisy has an offering for Mother. Do not spoil the moment!'

'Here you are, Grandma Bag,' squeaked Daisy. 'It's for you and it's a surprise because the other one got broke.'

The Bagthorpes watched numbly as Grandma pulled

off the wrappings. They knew well what to expect. Uncle Parker had obviously commissioned a second replica of the late and sainted Thomas, to replace the one that had crushed in a shower of maggots at the Family Reunion. As the final tissues fell aside their fears were confirmed. The present offering was if anything larger, gingerier and more malevolent-looking than its predecessor.

'It is beautiful!' cried Grandma predictably. 'Oh darling Daisy! The child is an angel!'

No one said anything to this, because the statement was not even debatable. Daisy was *not* an angel. She was on the contrary, as all the Bagthorpes knew to their cost, the inevitable harbinger and purveyor of doom. Her influence was such that Mr Bagthorpe had once suggested, in all seriousness, that what she really needed was exorcising. He had even offered to telephone the rector himself and arrange the ceremony.

'Desperate situations need desperate remedies,' he had asserted. 'Bell, book and candle is our last ditch.'

'It's from Arry Awk as well!' Daisy burbled, hopping from foot to foot, 'and we're going to look for a *real* Thomas for you, Daddy says.'

Grandma had no opportunity to voice her thanks to Arry Awk, even if she had been so disposed, because Mr Bagthorpe's oar was in in a flash.

'He is *what*?' he demanded.

'Thought it more or less my moral duty, d'you see,' explained Uncle Parker, who had been looking forward to observing Mr Bagthorpe's reaction to this news.

Uncle Parker's two main interests in life were driving round the countryside in a fast car like a bat out of hell, and goading Mr Bagthorpe. The former practice had resulted, some years previously, in the untimely death in the drive of Unicorn House of Thomas, a villainous ginger tom who had, Grandma maintained, been the light of her life. She also asserted that he was irreplaceable, which was why Uncle Parker had not immediately offered to re-place him.

He had (after allowing a suitable period of mourning) cunningly commissioned a pot life-sized replica of the original Thomas as a gift to Grandma, with the intention of following this up by the real thing. Nothing, he knew, would enrage Mr Bagthorpe more – even though he did not yet know that the latter had now embarked on a Master Plan for Survival in which there would be no place for non-productive livestock.

'Moral duty?' echoed Mr Bagthorpe incredulously. 'Moral –? Do you even know the *meaning* of the words?'

'I will look them up the moment I return home,' Uncle Parker promised. 'What do you say, Grandma? What about another shining purring jewel of a cat?'

'Aha!' yelled Mr Bagthorpe. '*Now* I've got it! Now I know what you're up to!'

Mr Bagthorpe, in his state of acute paranoia, and being alerted by certain key words in Uncle Parker's offer, had smelled a plot.

'It is a plot! A diabolical, malicious, well-laid plot!' he yelled. 'Think you'll kill two birds with one stone, don't you?'

'Er – which two birds were those, Henry?' queried Uncle Parker, delicately adjusting his cravat.

'My mother,' said Mr Bagthorpe carefully, making a real effort to control his voice and achieve Uncle Parker's kind of air of careless ease, 'has transferred her affections from that horrible dead cat to your daughter. Oh yes! Don't bother to deny it. It is common knowledge in this household, and strikes the fear of God into us all. What I suggest is that you, Russell, and you, Celia, are yourselves becoming uneasy about the situation. Though I may as well say that in my opinion your fears are groundless. In my opinion, Mother is more likely to fall under the pernicious influence of your accursed daughter than vice versa.'

'Russell!' wailed Aunt Celia faintly. 'Do not let him slander darling Daisy thus!'

'You will hear me out,' continued Mr Bagthorpe grimly. 'You have, as I say, become alarmed by the effects of this Unholy Alliance between the pair of them – and with just cause. *We're* all alarmed – some of us are nearly out of our minds. So what you are patently trying to do is re-transfer Mother's affection from your daughter back to another hell-ridden and malignant ginger tom. You will thus kill two birds with one stone. You will have put your own house in order, and at one and the same time thrown my own into purgatory.'

He paused for breath. His entire audience was listening fascinated to this laying bare of Uncle Parker's deepest motives. Jack was particularly interested in the way Mr Bagthorpe, whether consciously or not, avoided referring to Daisy by name. He did this with Zero as well. It helped him to pretend to himself that neither of them existed.

'Your scheme has failed,' Mr Bagthorpe then continued. 'It has been exposed. I am all for cutting off all relations between that pair, and indeed for your confining your daughter and her everlasting Arry Awk to your own premises in perpetuity. But if you seriously intend to acquire some non-productive, non-milk, egg or cheese-producing beast to add to this menage, then I am telling you, here and now, that the whole thing will boomerang on you, like *The Monkey's Paw.*'

He paused again.

'Which is – er – which is to say?' prompted Uncle Parker.

'Which is to say,' said Mr Bagthorpe triumphantly, 'that Mother, along with her Fortnum and Mason hamper and her familiar, will depart hence. She will go, Russell, to yourself and Celia.'

The company sat and pondered this ultimatum. In the resulting silence Daisy's voice, from somewhere outside, was heard. It was saying:

'Poor fing. Poor fing. Dusters to dusters and ashes to ashes!'

Mr Bagthorpe groaned.

Chapter Four

It later transpired that Daisy had now entered a new Phase. Uncle Parker called it a Morbid Phase, but Aunt Celia insisted that it was an Intimations of Mortality Phase. Under whatever label, what it meant, principally, was that Daisy was now holding funerals. Sometimes she held only one a day, at other times several. It depended mainly on what she could find to bury. She took these ceremonies very seriously, and tried as far as possible to dress for her part. On the present occasion, for instance, she had taken advantage of the disorganization in the kitchen to bear off a long Indian frock of Mrs Bagthorpe's that was airing on a rail, and a striped tea towel. She was swathed in the frock and wore the towel on her head. She said that she thought her outfit looked religious, and that vicars always wore long frocks.

What Daisy was burying no one thought to inquire at the time, as the ceremony was almost complete when they all rushed out to see what was happening. They stopped more or less in their tracks at the sight of Daisy in her borrowed vestments. She was scattering earth into a small hole and had real tears running down her face. There could be little doubt that this new Phase was a serious one.

'Goodbye, goodbye!' she wailed, flinging the last fistfuls of earth into the grave. 'Where are you gone now, poor little fing?'

This question struck her audience as rhetorical, and no one attempted to offer a reply.

'Darling child!' cried Aunt Celia, and she swayed forward to embrace her daughter, thereby collecting a good deal of damp soil on her own frock, and inciting Mr Bagthorpe's further wrath.

'Ye gods!' he exclaimed in disgust. 'What more must I endure? That child, Russell, is in urgent need of treatment. You are mad. She is mad.' Then, after a pause, 'They are mad.'

He was conjugating the verb to deaf ears.

'Come, Daisy,' Grandma said. 'You must not be upset. Come to my room, and you shall have some sugared almonds.'

Daisy instantly disengaged herself from her mother's embrace.

'I can't come, Grandma Bag,' she cried. 'I've got to do the *writing* yet.'

The writing was in fact one of the parts of her burials that Daisy enjoyed most. It meant composing a fitting epitaph for each of her various victims. She was very original in her choice of monuments, as the Bagthorpes were later to discover to their cost. Mr Bagthorpe said that the people who ran Highgate Cemetery could learn a lot from her. On this occasion she had appropriated a black non-stick baking sheet from Mrs Fosdyke's cupboard, and intended to chalk on it.

'You'll have to go away,' she told them all. 'I can't fink and write poems when there's people there.'

They all obediently trooped back indoors, and Mr Bagthorpe went straight into his study and banged the door.

'Poor Henry, he has no panache,' remarked Grandma. 'I shall accept the offer of a cat, Russell.'

'Really?' Uncle Parker was nonplussed. 'But do you *really* want to come and live at The Knoll?'

'I do not intend to,' she replied calmly, 'though I thank you for the invitation.'

'Correct me if I am wrong,' said Uncle Parker, 'but I was under the distinct impression that Henry laid down—'

'I care nothing for Henry and his idle threats,' Grandma told him. 'Next week, his Aunt Lucy is coming to visit. He is hoping, as you will know, to figure largely in her will. If he is seen as a man who drives helpless and ageing female relations out into the night, he will receive not a penny. Henry can be discounted. I shall have a cat, and I shall stop here.'

'But, Mother,' protested Mrs Bagthorpe weakly, 'you always said that Thomas was irreplaceable, and unique.'

She feared, as did her whole family, that Thomas had *not* been unique, and that a ginger tom quite as hateful and toothy would be produced.

'Time heals,' Grandma said sanctimoniously. 'I shall accept a substitute. I shall probably call him Thomas the Second. I shall establish a dynasty.'

'You'll have to train him to do something, Grandma,' Rosie told her. 'Father said we'd all got to do something.'

'Do I take it that Henry has gone off again at one of his unaccountable tangents?' asked Uncle Parker.

'Oh Russell, it is dreadful!' Mrs Bagthorpe told him. 'Henry has become quite unhinged at the sight of his latest bank statement, on which a large number of noughts had been printed in error. He has decided that we must become Self-Sufficient. He intends to till the soil and buy chickens and cook everything in straw. It is dreadful!'

'Cheer up, Laura. Ten to one the whole thing'll have blown over in a couple of days,' Uncle Parker inaccurately forecast. 'You know Henry. Who better? Where, by the way, is the ubiquitous Mrs Fosdyke?'

'Gone home,' William said glumly. 'Father told her to take the afternoon off.'

'And I've got to make a *blancmange*,' put in Tess disgustedly.

'And we've all got to live on rhubarb and beetroot until something else comes up,' wailed Rosie.

'Henry has said that we must dispense with Mrs Fosdyke's services,' Mrs Bagthorpe informed him. 'But I am absolutely against it. On this point I shall remain quite adamant. Without Mrs Fosdyke, there would be no Problems.'

'Well, well!' Uncle Parker was by now impressed by the way things were going. 'Henry is the last person on earth I should have thought of as Self-Sufficient. We must hope that the novelty will soon pall on him. In the meantime, Celia and myself will be delighted to slip you the odd food parcel, and so forth.'

They all thanked him fervently.

'We must now be on our way,' Uncle Parker said. 'We must find a second Thomas.'

Outside, Daisy seemed to be winding up her service. She was singing 'All Things Bright and Beautiful'.

'But cannot darling Daisy stop with me?' asked Grandma. Aunt Celia was not in favour of this.

'I cannot abandon my only child to a man who is raving,' she declared. 'And to who knows what unwholesome diet.'

'Nonsense, Celia!' Grandma said sharply. 'Henry is not raving. He is merely temporarily deranged, as he often is. And I do not imagine that we shall be reduced to a diet of rhubarb and beetroot in the immediate future. Surely the deep freeze and the larder are adequately stocked, Laura?'

'Of course,' replied Mrs Bagthorpe. 'As a matter of fact, I removed a chicken from the deep freeze only this morning, and shall casserole it tomorrow.'

The younger Bagthorpes cheered up considerably at this intelligence.

'Daisy will enjoy Mother's company, Celia dearest,' Uncle Parker told her. He had been subjected to a continuous procession of funerals in the past few days, and was ready for a rest from it.

Daisy herself then trotted in. She quickly pulled off the borrowed frock and tea towel and seemed all at once business-like again.

'That was a lovely funeral,' she told everyone. 'Poor little fing.'

Had the Bagthorpes not been in so bemused a state, they might have made inquiries as to whom or what Daisy had in fact been interring. When they did make the discovery, they were unanimous in heartily wishing *her* dead. On being asked whether she would like to stop at Unicorn House for a few days, she assented vigorously.

'You can help me with my funerals, Grandma Bag,' she offered generously. 'You can even dig.'

She waved a large, mud-covered serving spoon she had evidently also abstracted while the rest were preoccupied and off their guard.

'You can help me sow seeds, Daisy,' said Rosie, who was jealous of Daisy's friendship with Grandma. 'Then, when they've grown, you can help me pick things.'

'Are you not being a little optimistic?' said Tess. 'I know of no seeds other than cress that can be sown and harvested within the week. However, I have a paranormal experiment I wish to conduct, and will use your seeds as guniea-pigs, so to speak.'

The Parkers then departed, and the Unholy Alliance went up to Grandma's room for a conference. Mr Bagthorpe emerged from his study shortly afterwards, brandishing a rota he had drawn up. During his absence, Mrs Bagthorpe had told her off-spring that she thought it best if, at any rate for the time being, they co-operated with him.

'Russell may well be right,' she said hopefully, 'and this will turn out to be a mere whim, or a Passing Phase.'

Mrs Bagthorpe had a strong tendency to Positive Thinking, and believed touchingly in its power. The thoroughness with which Mr Bagthorpe had already plotted his Plan for Survival did not strike any of the others as looking much like a whim. It bore all the hallmarks of an all-out Bagthorpian obsession.

William was despatched on a bus to Aysham with orders to return with every single library book he could lay his hands on related to market gardening, chicken rearing, pig keeping, household economics and so forth. Every member of the family had to send back his or her current loans, whether or not they had been read.

'We need every ticket we possess,' Mr Bagthorpe told them. 'And moreover, there will in future be no time for people to lie around reading library books. We shall be peasants. Peasants do not lie around reading library books.'

Rosie was dismissed with strict instructions to dispose forthwith of the Great Bagthorpe Daisy Chain still draped about the garden. Her protests were useless.

'There will be no room for anything ornamental in this garden,' he announced. 'That chain is neither use nor ornament. The front lawn will be ploughed up.'

Mrs Bagthorpe opened her mouth to protest about this but closed it again, remembering that she was supposed to appear to co-operate. She sat breathing very deeply as her husband continued.

'You, Tess, can go and clear all the rubble out of the summer house. Hens do not require deckchairs and parasols, and nor shall we, from now on. You, Jack, can get a spade and dig up the strawberry bed.'

Mrs Bagthorpe opened her mouth again, and closed it.

'Strawberries are a luxury we can no longer afford,' he continued. 'A large area of ground is devoted to a crop that is unproductive for eleven months out of twelve. We shall now rotate crops. We shall plant potatoes there. Get started, the lot of you. I shall go back to my desk and work out further details.'

'What shall I do?' asked Mrs Bagthorpe faintly.

'Make some chutney,' he advised her. 'Pickle some beetroot. Anything.'

'Just a minute,' William said. 'What about Grandma and Grandpa? What're *they* doing?'

'The former will be worse than useless to us,' replied his father. 'The most we can hope for is eventually to starve her out. And I do not at present have time to explain to Father what is happening.'

Grandpa was deaf, but nobody was sure to quite what degree. Uncle Parker maintained that he was S D – Selectively Deaf. This meant that he heard, in effect, what he wanted to hear. In that case, Jack thought, it was likely that Grandpa never would understand what was now going on. He would not *want* to know.

The family scattered on its respective missions. Jack found his own task depressing.

'I think it's really terrible, digging up strawberries,' he told Zero, who lay watching him. 'You wouldn't know, old chap, but they're really nice. Especially with cream. I wonder if goats have cream?'

Tess kept going past, staggering under armfuls of deckchairs and other garden furniture. She seemed to be carrying on a muttered, incomprehensible monologue. Jack thought it probable that she was swearing in French.

Every now and then Rosie trundled mournfully by with a wheelbarrow full of rapidly decomposing daisies.

'I shall still do a mural anyway!' she yelled defiantly on one such trip. 'I don't need to *see* the daisies. I can imagine them.'

Jack felt sympathetic towards this project.

'The only thing is, Rosie,' he said, 'what about paints? I mean, how many have you got left?'

'Why?' she demanded, staring.

'Because,' Jack told her wisely, 'Father is never going to let you buy any. You can't eat them, you see. They're non-productive. What I think you ought to do is start looking for berries and barks and things, like the cavemen did. You ought to get some wood and stuff.'

Rosie seemed impressed by this advice, and was evidently acting on it, because after the final load of daisies had been wheeled by, Jack caught occasional glimpses of her squeezing flowers between her fingers, or piggling at the bark of trees. He felt quite pleased and flattered by this.

'P'raps you and me are going to be quite good at this Survival thing,' he told an apparently uninterested Zero. 'If I get really good at it, it'd count as a String to my Bow. I bet Father'd let me count it.'

Jack had never quite given up hoping that one day he would have Strings to his Bow, like the others. He knew that he was not, and never would be, outstandingly clever or talented, but it seemed to him that he might well be good at Surviving. He was no more attracted than anyone else by the prospect of living on lettuce and water, and working his fingers to the bone. But if the thing was inevitable, he thought he might as well throw himself into it wholeheartedly. He could at least be on level terms with his siblings. Survival, he could see, was a great equalizer.

When the Bagthorpes forgathered at tea-time, only Jack himself, Mr Bagthorpe and the Unholy Alliance could be described as anything near cheerful. Everyone else looked tired and sullen. (Grandpa had gone fishing with firm instructions from Mr Bagthorpe to catch as many as possible large, edible fish.) Tess said that she had almost certainly slipped a disc carrying deckchairs, and would never be able to perform a Judo fall again. Rosie's arms and hands were indelibly stained with murky shades of crimson and tan, and bore a network of scratches. Mrs Bagthorpe had been making chutney and the whole ground floor smelled of hot vinegar. The food itself was hardly appetizing. Tess had forgotten about the blancmange until late afternoon, and it was still warm, as well as unmistakably watery. Even Mr Bagthorpe had to force it down.

'This will be a tonic to us all,' he informed his unconvinced audience. 'We have been taking in far too much cholesterol. We shall soon reap the benefits in increased mental alertness and bodily vigour. Our brains are all furred up with cholesterol.'

Mr Bagthorpe was not really very strong on dietetics, and never succeeded in acquiring any sort of mastery of the subject. He used the expression 'furring up' a lot, and said that most modern foods did this, ranging from white bread through tinned fruit to ice cream. The opposite of these, and therefore beneficial to the system, were commodities that 'thin your blood down' According to him dandelion leaves did this, and also beetroot, rhubarb, and neat whisky. He was almost as confused as Mrs Fosdyke herself about vitamins, and maintained that they were 'alive'. He said this was why fruit should be eaten fresh. It was no good eating it, he said, when the vitamins were 'dead'. It could even be harmful. 'You would not wish to digest the contents of a charnel house,' he told them, 'and that is what you do when you eat a wizened apple.'

He also immovably contended that tea and coffee both stained your insides brown, and were detrimental to health. When the others said that they did not care what colour their insides were, he launched into a long and stern lecture about the way England had started to go downhill after the introduction into the country of these enervating foreign beverages.

'The honest English yeoman quaffed only ale, in large quantities,' he declared. 'It is how the British character was formed.'

This was lucky for Mr Bagthorpe, since he was the only member of the family who enjoyed drinking beer. (He was later, and with disastrous consequences, to begin brewing his own.) He told them to drink at least a gallon a day of water, which was full of oxygen, and would invigorate them. When they voiced their doubts about this theory, he asked triumphantly how, in that case, fish managed to survive? As piscatology was a String to nobody's Bow, the family were for the time being unable to come up with a satisfactory answer to this, though they were convinced there was one.

During this first meal since the Plan for Survival had been put into operation, Mr Bagthorpe was not yet fully into his stride about food values, and even let Tess open a tin of peaches, saying that the sooner such tainted food was eaten and out of the way, the better. He was beginning, Jack thought, to sound dangerously like the Sainted Aunt. The only difference was that the latter really believed in vegetarianism, whereas Mr Bagthorpe was just out to save money.

As they were stolidly making their way through this depressing meal, the telephone rang. Mrs Bagthorpe went out into the hall to answer it, and returned quite soon.

'An exact date has been fixed for Aunt Lucy's visit,' she announced. 'She is to arrive the day after tomorrow. I said that you, Henry, would meet her at the station at twelve noon.'

Nobody brightened perceptibly at this news.

'She didn't say anything about grated carrots and nuts,

and such, did she?' William asked hopefully. If Great Aunt Lucy liked food of a rich and unwholesome sort, then with any luck, the whole family would benefit.

'Not a word,' his mother told him.

The younger Bagthorpes reverted to gloom.

'If you ask me,' said Rosie dolefully, more or less voicing the thoughts of them all, 'this family's got a curse on it. Nothing ever goes right.'

'I agree,' Mr Bagthorpe told her. 'I am glad that you can see this. I am not so paranoiac as I first feared. The whole world is ranged up against us out there. But we shall defy it. We shall gird up our loins. We shall survive.'

Chapter Five

The following day Mrs Bagthorpe made a point of rising and going downstairs early, to be sure of seeing Mrs Fosdyke and explaining the situation before Mr Bagthorpe himself came down. She was not at all certain how she was going to do this explaining, and spent longer than usual on her Yoga and Breathing in the hope that they would stand her in good stead during the forthcoming ordeal. It seemed to Mrs Bagthorpe that it was going to be no easy matter to explain the situation in such a way that it would not sound lunatic.

It was unfortunate that Mrs Fosdyke herself was in no mood for receiving news of a direful and unsettling nature. She had remembered, while tossing restlessly during the night, certain fragments of Mr Bagthorpe's description of life as lived by Aunt Lucy in Torquay. She *thought* she had remembered these, but turning them over in her mind as she scurried from the village in the cold light of day, she felt that she must have remembered wrongly.

'Nobody could be that downright mad,' she told herself, though without real conviction.

What Mr Bagthorpe had said was that Aunt Lucy did not believe in Time, and accordingly tried to sabotage it. One of her methods of doing this was to have several clocks in every room of her considerable mansion, all showing different times. The combined incessant ticking, chiming and ringing of these were, he had said, a refined form of the Chinese water torture. A further inconvenience occasioned by this particular Bee in Aunt Lucy's bonnet, was that there were no regular mealtimes. She tried to fool the Time by dodging about with these, and it was no unusual thing, he said, if she were in a particularly perky mood, to find oneself tucking into buttered crumpets and China tea at eleven thirty at night, after the test card on television had disappeared and given way to a high-pitched whine. He had also, he claimed, been served with grilled kippers and toast at three in the afternoon, following on the heels of a supper served only an hour previously. Whether she had Time on the hop he did not know, he said, but judging by his own disorientation, it seemed likely.

'When the final trump sounds,' he said, 'it will be centuries ahead of schedule, and brought on by Aunt Lucy.'

Mrs Fosdyke had further memories of accounts of Mr Bagthorpe's nocturnal battles with the clocks ranged about his own room. He had buried clocks in drawers, stuffed socks into the works, and attempted to bend the chimes. On one occasion he had returned home with two of Aunt Lucy's alarm clocks, which he had wrapped in his dressing-gown and stowed in his suitcase in an attempt to muffle their particularly penetrating ticks. Fortunately, such was the plethora of timepieces in the house, these had not been missed, and he had been able to smuggle them back (wound down) on a subsequent visit.

None of this was any comfort to Mrs Fosdyke. As she hedgehogged along she prepared a speech to Mrs Bagthorpe in which she would make clear that in this matter there would be no co-operation forthcoming from herself.

'If they think I'm coming in to fry bacon at midnight and be serving roasts and three veg at dawn, then they'll have to look elsewhere,' she thought. '*And* I shall have to make inquiries about the full moon.'

Aunt Lucy, she definitely recalled, was affected by the moon, and knew it. Mr Bagthorpe had given descriptions of how she would roam about the house blocking out every chink of light, and stuffing dusters into cracks, and as often as not would sleep through the daytime during critical phases, so that she could be wide awake during the hours of darkness and able to fend off the sinister influences of the moon's rays. (This, of course, fooled the Time, too.)

Mrs Fosdyke was no expert on madness, despite her years with the Bagthorpes, but did know that lunacy was connected with the full moon. She was an addict of Dracula and Frankenstein films, but preferred her madness and horror on a screen, safely partitioned from life as actually lived. She harboured no ambitions to meet mad persons roaming about with hatchets and newly grown incisors.

'It's no part of my duties,' she told herself firmly. She knew she would have to stand her ground very firmly when she confronted the Bagthorpes.

Mrs Bagthorpe, then, was already in the kitchen making herself a fortifying cup of coffee when Mrs Fosdyke entered, her lately rehearsed speech still fresh in her mind.

'Ah, good morning, Mrs Fosdyke,' Mrs Bagthorpe greeted her with a determined smile, behind which, had she been a student of human nature, Mrs Fosdyke would have detected desperation.

'Good morning, I'm sure,' she parried, in tones that implied that it was not, of course, anything of the sort. She went scooting through her routine of whipping off coat and headscarf and exchanging shoes for slippers, and Mrs Bagthorpe waited apprehensively.

'Ah!' she exclaimed brightly, as Mrs Fosdyke approached the sink for the first skirmish of the day with the dishes. 'I was hoping to have a word with you, Mrs Fosdyke.'

'I was hoping to have one with you, as well, Mrs Bagthorpe,' countered Mrs Fosdyke. 'About that old woman at Torquay.'

'Ah, well, I think I can answer your query about that,'

Mrs Bagthorpe told her smilingly. 'She is to arrive tomorrow, at noon, and will be here in good time for luncheon.'

'Time for lunch for some it might be,' said Mrs Fosdyke ominously. 'Time for lunch for ordinary mortals, I dare say.'

'Why, whatever do you mean?' cried Mrs Bagthorpe. 'Surely we normally take luncheon at one?'

'*You* do,' Mrs Fosdyke told her. 'It's that old woman. Roast and three veg in the middle of the night, Mr Bagthorpe said. I heard him. Only last time he went there. And buttered crumpets in the —'

'Oh really!' exclaimed Mrs Bagthorpe, with an attempt at a gay laugh. 'Surely you did not take that seriously? Surely you know Mr Bagthorpe's little jokes by now?'

'Oh, I know them, all right,' Mrs Fosdyke agreed, 'and not funny, neither, most of 'em. I shall have to give notice, Mrs Bagthorpe, that I shall be putting meals on tables at the times I always have. I take a pride in my meals, Mrs Bagthorpe, as you know.'

'Indeed, yes!' said Mrs Bagthorpe fervently, her brow clouding a little as she thought of the news she had herself to impart regarding meals that were to be variations on a theme of spring onions, lettuce, beetroot and rhubarb. 'So that is quite settled, Mrs Fosdyke.'

'That's all right, then,' assented Mrs Fosdyke grudgingly. 'She won't be stopping long, will she?'

'Oh I am sure not,' Mrs Bagthorpe assured her. 'Just for a day or two. She is quite elderly, you know — eighty-seven — and at that age, of course, there is no place like home.'

She felt pleased with this last speech which sounded, even to her own ears, reassuring and sensible in the manner of Stella Bright.

'Because there's a full moon on the eleventh,' continued

Mrs Fosdyke in dark tones, and on what seemed to Mrs Bagthorpe a quite inconsequential tack.

'Really?' Mrs Bagthorpe replied politely. She then made a determined effort to steer the conversation into the channels she had herself intended. 'What I really wanted to have a word with you about, was one or two changes in household arrangements.'

'Oh yes?' said Mrs Fosdyke unhelpfully.

'The fact of the matter is,' began Mrs Bagthorpe delicately, 'that household expenses have been rather heavy of late. And what with inflation, and the cost of living, and one thing and another, my husband and I think it advisable to make certain changes.'

'Oh yes?' said Mrs Fosdyke again. If the foregoing had been the introduction to her own dismissal, she was certainly not going to help matters along.

'For one thing, we thought we should make more extensive use of garden produce,' said Mrs Bagthorpe brightly.

'And what would that be?' inquired Mrs Fosdyke, beginning to set out plates and cutlery in preparation for breakfast.

'Well, to begin with, there is a row of perfectly delicious cos lettuce,' commenced Mrs Bagthorpe.

'Oh yes?'

'And then... then there is some beetroot. Which, of course, can either be eaten in a salad, or pickled.'

On this Mrs Fosdyke made no comment. Encouraged, Mrs Bagthorpe went on.

'Then there are some spring onions, I believe. And a very large crop of rhubarb.'

Mrs Fosdyke turned and faced her employer.

'Is it salad you're wanting tonight, then?' she asked. 'And stewed rhubarb with custard?'

'Well – yes, certainly,' Mrs Bagthorpe floundered. 'But –

not *only* tonight. Quite frequently, you understand. Until we have exhausted the supplies.'

In the silence that followed, Mrs Bagthorpe thought helplessly that she would have to postpone the matter of cooking everything in straw to a later occasion. There was clearly a limit to how much Mrs Fosdyke was going to take in at present.

'Often,' said Mrs Fosdyke at length. 'You mean you want 'em often?'

'That is quite right, Mrs Fosdyke,' affirmed Mrs Bagthorpe with relief. 'And of course we shall immediately begin to grow other crops, to make for a more varied and nutritious menu.'

She decided to stop short of the cow and chickens for the time being too.

'There won't be a deal you can do with them,' Mrs Fosdyke observed with perfect truth. 'You can't do much ringing the changes with beetroot and rhubarb.'

'That I quite understand,' Mrs Bagthorpe agreed, 'and you will certainly not find us unappreciative of your efforts to do so.'

'Well, up to you, of course.' Mrs Fosdyke shrugged her shoulders. 'You'll not be going vegitinarian, I hope?'

'Oh, *indeed* not!' Mrs Bagthorpe was glad that she could wholeheartedly make this assurance at least. 'As a matter of fact, I took a chicken out of the deep freeze only yesterday, and thought we would casserole it for lunch.'

'Hmm. Best get started on that, then,' Mrs Fosdyke said.

She went into the pantry and began to rummage about for her ingredients, and Mrs Bagthorpe, with a sigh of relief, sank back and began to drink her coffee.

'Things will not be so bad, after all,' she told herself Positively. 'The worst is now over.'

It was not.

'Where did you say you'd put that chicken?' Mrs

Fosdyke's voice broke into Mrs Bagthorpe's self-congratulatory reverie.

'What? Oh – the chicken. Surely – on the side, Mrs Fosdyke.'

She rose.

'At least, I think...' she eyed dubiously the empty work-top. 'I may have put it in the fridge, later... we had rather a trying day yesterday. Now where...?'

She stooped to examine the contents of the refrigerator.

'Extraordinary...' she murmured. Mrs Fosdyke had gone back into the pantry.

'Not in 'ere!' she called. 'Found it, 'ave you?'

'No. No, I have not,' admitted Mrs Bagthorpe. 'But the whole thing is quite absurd. I removed the chicken from the deep freeze, I placed it – I placed it somewhere *here* ... and then...' her voice trailed away. She really had no inkling of the bird's movements beyond this juncture.

Mr Bagthorpe then entered, followed closely by Jack and William.

'Ah, Henry!' his wife greeted him. 'Perhaps you can throw some light on the matter.'

'What matter?' he demanded ungraciously.

'Mrs Fosdyke and I have mislaid a chicken,' she told him.

'And what, Laura, in the name of all that is wonderful, do you suppose *I* would do with a chicken?' he asked her.

'Well – nothing, of course, dear,' she faltered. 'I simply thought...'

'Simply nothing,' came the terse rejoinder. 'In this house nothing is simple.'

'No, dear, of course not. But it *is* all such a mystery. You see, I moved this chicken from the deep freeze, and I placed it –'

'When?' interrupted William. He, in company with Jack was more interested in the whereabouts of the missing chicken than was their father. They had both dreamed of it, a gravied oasis in a desert of lettuce and beetroot.

'Yesterday morning.' She was becoming a little desperate. 'I remember it quite distinctly. You may have noticed it standing on the side youself, Mrs Fosdyke?'

'I might've,' Mrs Fosdyke said non-committally. 'I can't say I remember.'

'But I did, I definitely did,' Mrs Bagthorpe insisted. 'I *mentioned* it, you may remember?'

'You mentioned it, all right,' Jack told her reassuringly. 'You said you were going to put it in a casserole.'

'That's right! There!' she cried gratefully.

Her husband favoured her with a cool stare.

'Then where *have* you put it, Laura?' he inquired. 'Could it be that you have casseroled it already, and forgotten?'

'Oh Henry, do be *serious*!' Mrs Bagthorpe tried at all times to keep her sense of perspective, but could feel it now blurring into virtual invisibility.

'Let's do a recap,' William intervened. 'Reconstruct the thing. You took the chicken out in the morning. Right?'

'Right,' his mother agreed

'And Mrs Fosdyke did not witness this, so at present we have only your word for it. Mrs Fosdyke went home.'

'I never asked to!' Mrs Fosdyke put in loudly.

'We then had lunch. As we finished, Uncle Parker came.'

'And Aunt Celia. *And* Daisy,' Jack said.

There was a sudden chill pause.

'*And* Daisy,' Jack repeated.

'Who held a funeral,' William supplied in flat tones. He sat down suddenly.

'But *surely* . . .?' Mrs Bagthorpe faltered. 'Oh – I'm sure you are wrong!'

Followed closely by Jack, she hurried to the outer door, to Mrs Fosdyke's extreme mystification.

Jack and his mother stood and stared at Daisy's epitaph, chalked on to a non-stick black baking sheet:

> Higledy pigledy pore ded hen
> Yore fethers will nevver cum back agen.
> 1763–1800

Jack read this inscription out loud, to convince himself.

'Oh my God!' Mr Bagthorpe was now behind them. 'Even unto the grave!'

William and Mrs Fosdyke had now joined them round the newly dug grave.

'Whatever . . . ? That's my best non-stick baking –!' Mrs Fosdyke snatched up the monument and began to wipe off the inscription with her wrap-around pinafore. Jack, oddly, found himself fleetingly shocked by this desecration.

'So our dinner is under there, we can take it?' said Mr Bagthorpe unnecessarily. There could be no escaping this conclusion.

'The bird was, after all, dead,' said Mrs Bagthorpe feebly, 'and to the child it must have seemed the most natural thing in the world to bury it. She was weeping, Henry.'

'*I* am almost weeping,' he informed her, unmoved by this reminder of his niece's tenderheartedness. 'I shall telephone Russell at once.'

He left the graveside, cursing under his breath. It occurred to Jack that while it had been his father's idea to follow a policy of eating spring onions and rhubarb, he could hardly have been looking forward to this, any more than anybody else. The casseroled chicken must have appeared to him, too, a welcome landmark in such a diet.

'You mean to say,' came the disbelieving voice of Mrs Fosdyke (who did not, after all, know that Daisy had gone into a new Phase of Intimations of Mortality), 'that that Daisy's dug that bird into the *soil*?'

'I – I fear so, Mrs Fosdyke,' Mrs Bagthorpe told her faintly. 'But we must try not to be too harsh in our judgement. The bird was, after all, dead, and must have appeared to her –'

'You've already said that Mother,' said William coldly. What he really wished was that the hen was in the casserole, and Daisy in the grave.

'I don't believe –!' came Mrs Fosdyke's voice flatly. 'Here!' She bent, and began to scrabble at the earth with her fingers.

'Ugh!' she screeched, and fell back.

Gleaming through the disturbed soil was the nude, pale pink and mottled skin of what was, unmistakably, an oven-ready chicken.

Mrs Bagthorpe shuddered. Even Jack felt as if he would never be able to face a cooked chicken again. He had never thought of one as a corpse before. He, too, wished Daisy dead and buried.

Mrs Fosdyke stood stockstill, goggling with shock.

'I don't believe it!' she said at last. And then, genuinely mystified, 'That Daisy – wherever does she get her ideas?'

'I don't know, Mrs Fosdyke,' replied Mrs Bagthorpe truthfully. 'She is certainly a most original child.'

'Original!' Mrs Fosdyke was disgusted.

'Original *and* tiresome,' qualified Mrs Bagthorpe, though Jack could see that from Mrs Fosdyke's point of view, even this description came nowhere near doing justice to the case.

'It'll have to *stop* buried, that is certain,' remarked Mrs Fosdyke. 'And what'll you be having with the veg, Mrs Bagthorpe? And it's to be hoped that dog of yours don't go ferreting down there and dragging chickens with soil on into my kitchen.'

'He won't,' Jack promised. 'He doesn't like digging things up.'

When the news of Daisy's latest exercise in creativity spread to the rest of the household, feelings ran high. Only Grandma, possibly feeling secure in the prospect of a Fortnum and Mason hamper, seemed unmoved by it.

'Celia has unwittingly produced a genius,' she told the others. 'You had better look to your laurels.'

Daisy herself was very upset by the hostile reaction to her funeral, and about having her gravestone removed and wiped.

'Poor little dead fing!' she sobbed. 'He was all cold and pimply and no feathers. Nobody cares!'

This was not strictly true. The Bagthorpes did care, deeply. Attitudes towards Daisy hardened further. To be ranged up against the whole world was in itself a considerable prospect, but now, it appeared, there was a saboteur within their very walls. The outlook ahead was bleak.

Chapter Six

Before setting off to meet Aunt Lucy at the station, Mr Bagthorpe gathered his family together and gave them a thorough briefing.

'Have it clear in your minds,' he told them, 'that our whole future as a united family depends on this visit.'

'*Are* we united?' William asked.

'That is precisely the kind of unwarranted levity we can do without in the present crisis,' his father told him. 'We are united in the sense that we are, as yet, under one roof. Unless Aunt Lucy comes up with a fairly hefty contribution in the fairly near future, we shall be split up and sent to the four corners of the earth. We shall have to throw our lives upon the State.'

'Oh *Henry*!' his wife protested. 'Surely you are exaggerating!'

'Your trouble, Laura,' he told her, 'is that you have a congenital predisposition to look on the bright side of things. It is lucky that you have me to redress the balance. Furthermore, you will all show signs of determination and strength of character, whether or not you possess them.'

Jack wondered exactly how one should behave in order to be seen to possess these qualities, but did not like to ask.

'As for you,' he addressed himself to Grandma now, 'you will forthwith desist from perpetually throwing spanners into the works. You will be polite and gracious to someone who is, after all, a full ten years older than yourself, and a lady to boot.'

'I do not require advice from you on how to conduct

myself,' she replied coldly. 'I, of course, do not stand to benefit from behaving in a slavish and ingratiating fashion. It is fortunate, therefore, that I am possessed of naturally impeccable taste and manners.'

'And as for your protégée,' he continued, meaning Daisy, 'try to get through to her that this is not a public cemetery. Aunt Lucy, at her age, will not be entertained by a continual procession of funerals. Or cremations,' he added as a wise afterthought.

'I do not propose to fetter Daisy's creative urges,' Grandma returned. 'I would not want the responsibility. If *I* can contemplate the enactment of a funeral with equanimity, then so should this other person be able to.'

Mr Bagthorpe, knowing the futility of arguing the point further, stomped out of the house, leaving his already battered family to put themselves together. No one was very clear what part they were supposed to be playing. They had been given to understand, on the one hand, that Great Aunt Lucy's every wish was to be pandered to. On the other, they had been told to display determination and strength of character – which meant, presumably, that they were to press on with the rhubarb and beetroot aspect of things. The two policies seemed irreconcilable – unless, of course, the old lady turned out to be a devotee of a diet of unalleviated salad and stewed rhubarb.

'I think we ought to have meals as usual while she's here,' William told his mother as soon as Mr Bagthorpe had driven off. 'Aunt Lucy'll never leave us anything if she has to eat all that muck.'

'I agree,' Tess said surprisingly. She never agreed with William about anything unless her back was truly to the wall. 'Gastronomic considerations should override all others. I can easily demonstrate my own strength of character by conversing with her in French and Danish, and by playing arpeggios on my oboe.'

'I think we should try to strike a balance,' said Mrs Bagthorpe sensibly. 'It is, after all, summer, and the season for salads.'

'Which don't have to be kept hot,' put in Mrs Fosdyke, who still had misgivings about the Time aspect of things.

'Exactly,' Mrs Bagthorpe agreed. 'And do remember, everybody, that we are *humouring* your father. The thing will burn itself out if we give it the least chance.'

She sounded a good deal more like Stella Bright than she felt. She alone had seen the sheaf of stamped addressed envelopes on her husband's desk. They had been addressed to bodies like the Milk Marketing Board, the Council for the Preservation of Rural England and the *Farmer and Stockbreeder*. Mr Bagthorpe was not in the habit of wasting stamps, even without benefit of an overdraft running, as he professed still to believe, into untold figures.

It was very unfortunate that one of Rosie's hamsters was found dead immediately after Mr Bagthorpe's departure. It was William who made this discovery. He had gone into one of the disused stables in search of a length of cable, and his eye chanced to fall on the cages in which the hamsters were kept. He looked at them because at the time they were producing a noticeable degree of noise. Several of the hamsters were busy exercising themselves by running non-stop on their wheels. William, whose mind was currently occupied with devising methods of producing free electricity, cast a thoughtful eye upon them.

'A treadmill,' he murmured to himself. 'A windmill generates electricity, and so could a treadmill. If we could devise a means of harnessing the energy expended by the hamsters in treading those wheels, then we –'

He was halted on the threshold of a scientific breakthrough by observing a limp and furry shape to the fore of one of the cages. He advanced to investigate.

His half-formed theory was nipped in the bud. Clearly hamsters were not up to treading treadmills on any full-time, regular basis. This one had obviously died of a heart attack after its exertions.

'Better tell Rosie,' he decided.

He did so without taking due thought. He might have known, he told himself bitterly later, that Rosie would go straight to tell Daisy of the death by misadventure. Rosie truly loved Daisy, and thought her sweet and funny, and used every means in her power to lure her away from Grandma's side whenever possible.

The result was that Mr Bagthorpe, later in the morning, motoring sedately up the drive with Aunt Lucy beside him, came close to a head-on collision with a funeral procession. It consisted of Daisy wearing a trailing black crocheted shawl and felt hat of Grandma's, followed by Rosie and Grandma herself, both suitably attired in deep mourning, and carrying flowers. It had been Grandma's idea to inter the hamster in the front garden, rather than the back, because she had secretly hoped for the confrontation that in fact now took place. She was exceedingly pleased with this outcome. It established herself in the eyes of the visitor as dauntingly and possibly unbeatably eccentric, and it goaded Mr Bagthorpe into a towering rage. Round one, Grandma thought with satisfaction, had definitely gone to her.

Mr Bagthorpe had to pull up quite sharply to avoid a situation that would have involved at least one real funeral, if not three. Jack heard the gravel scatter, and approached cautiously behind the screen of laurels to observe the scene. He looked first, naturally, at Great Aunt Lucy, to see if she would be how he had imagined her. In fact, her face was the least noticeable thing about her, sandwiched as it was between a large beflowered hat, and a chest crowded with lace and a good number of shining ornaments. (These later turned out to be brooch watches, all set at different times.)

The most striking figure present was undoubtedly Grandma, who was wearing a black bonnet and veil that she had kept for nearly half a century in case she ever wanted to take up bee-keeping again. None of her fea-

tures were even faintly discernible under this thick veil, and Jack wondered how she could see where she was going. Rosie had struck a more casual note in a black leotard and tights, but evidently thought the addition of a hat necessary to the solemnity of the occasion, and wore low over her eyes a greenish-black homburg, presumably the property of Grandpa.

The members of this procession were singing a kind of dirge, or even three separate dirges. When Mr Bagthorpe wound down his window and started shouting they were not deflected from their course. They appeared to give only the briefest of glances in his direction, and then made slowly off over the far lawn, presenting an eerie picture in the brilliant midday sun. Jack himself was torn between following the car to the house, and attending the funeral. He decided on the latter course. A funeral was less of an everyday occurrence than the spectacle of Mr Bagthorpe shouting.

He caught up with the cortège just as it halted by what was clearly to be the final resting place of Rosie's hamster. Daisy was carrying a chocolate box. She placed it reverently under a lilac bush, and Jack guessed that it contained the corpse. She then delved under her layers of shawl and skirts and produced a trowel.

'You better sing another verse while I'm digging,' she told the other mourners, and herself set to work in a businesslike way with the trowel. A hole soon materialized.

'Now,' said Daisy with satisfaction. 'Now it's the proper part. Oh dear, poor little mouse!'

'Hamster,' Rosie told her, sniffing. 'His name was Truffles.'

Daisy held aloft the chocolate box for a moment, in the manner of a magician inviting an audience to inspect a receptacle from which he is about to produce a dozen white doves.

'Goodbye, Truffles!' she said. Tears were already beginning to roll down her cheeks. Evidently a long personal relationship with the deceased was not necessary in order for her to experience deep feelings of bereavement.

'There you go now, for ever and ever, down into the soil for ever and ever!'

She bent and placed the box in the hole.

'Ashes to ashes, dusters to dusters,' she cried loudly, scattering handfuls of soil over the coffin.

Jack was unable to judge the strength of Grandma's emotions behind her black curtain, but Rosie was by now sobbing in earnest. She herself moved in and threw some soil.

'Goodbye, Truffles,' she sobbed.

'Poor dead Truffles,' agreed Daisy. 'For ever and ever,' she added, evidently feeling that these words had a strong ecclesiastical ring.

The hole filled in, Daisy straightened up.

'Now we'll sing hymn four thousand and ninety-six,' she announced. '"We Plough The Fields and Scatter."'

Jack thought this choice curious, but supposed that Daisy had only a limited repertoire of hymns. Her congregation obediently struck up, and Jack thought how amazing it was that Grandma should be so docile and allow Daisy to take the leading role. Usually if Grandma was involved in anything, she insisted on running it.

The trio sang nearly half 'We Plough The Fields and Scatter' before they trailed off for lack of words.

'Amen,' Daisy said. 'That'll do. Now we've got to do the flowers and writing.'

She again delved into her robes and produced what looked like a large, slender volume, with a message printed on it in yellow. This she pushed at something of an angle into the soil at the head of the grave.

'I seen books in the graveyard,' Daisy told the others. 'Books are good. Now put the flowers on.'

Grandma and Rosie then advanced with their bunches of flowers and each in turn placed her tribute under the headstone.

'For ever and ever amen,' Daisy said, terminating the ceremony. 'We better go and have dinner now. Goodbye, poor dead mouse.'

'Hamster,' Rosie told her again.

Jack waited until the mourners had disappeared from sight, then advanced to inspect the grave. The headstone, he noted with misgivings, was Mr Bagthorpe's Road Atlas. It bore the inscription:

> Here lies a mous
> In a holey hous
> But the pore dead thing
> Will here the bels ring
> 1692–1792
> Forevver and evver.

'That's oil paint she's used,' Jack thought. 'It'll never come off. Father'll kill her.'

He was reminded by this that Mr Bagthorpe would at that moment almost certainly be in murderous mood, and hastened back to the house to witness this.

He was not disappointed. The funeral procession had arrived just before him, and was being introduced to Aunt Lucy by Mrs Bagthorpe. Her husband had his mouth so tightly closed that it was virtually invisible. Great Aunt Lucy herself was sitting like a ramrod, her eyes fixed on Grandma – the only person present in whom she appeared to have any interest. Anyone handing out a prize for fancy dress would have been bound to give it to Grandma.

'Charmed,' Great Aunt Lucy was saying. 'May I inquire how old you are?'

'I am seventy-five,' Grandma replied, 'although of course I am aware that I look twenty years younger.'

'I should have put you at eighty,' Aunt Lucy said. 'I myself am eighty-seven. Or rather, I would be, if I believed in Time, which I am happy to say I do not.'

'Nor, perhaps, shall I,' parried Grandma, 'when I reach your age.'

Mrs Bagthorpe helplessly watched this exchange, which by no means, even to a confirmed Positive Thinker, seemed to augur well.

'Why are you wearing that ugly bonnet?' Great Aunt Lucy then inquired, fingering her own chiffon roses.

'I do not normally wear hats,' replied Grandma imperturbably, 'which are these days considered vulgar and dated. Today, however, I have been attending a funeral, and naturally observed the niceties.'

'We been burying a mouse,' Daisy piped up. 'He was Truffles and now he's dusters to dusters and ashes to ashes. *That* hat's got a lot of flowers!'

Mr Bagthorpe now unclenched his facial muscles.

'That child, I am profoundly grateful to say, is not my own. It belongs to Celia and Russell. The only reason it is in this house at all is because Mother invited it. I advise you to give the pair of them a wide berth. They are –'

'And this is Rosie,' interrupted Mrs Bagthorpe hastily. 'She is nine, but already has Several Strings to her Bow, don't you, dear? Perhaps she will paint your Portrait while you are with us.'

'And who is that?' inquired the old lady, ignoring this suggestion.

'This is Jack,' Mrs Bagthorpe told her.

'And what does *he* do?'

'I don't do anything, Great Aunt Lucy,' Jack told her. 'I'm very pleased to meet you, and hope you will have a happy visit. Does your dog fight?'

He had left Zero up in his room, on Mr Bagthorpe's instructions.

'If that infernal hound eats that accursed Peke, we're finished,' he said.

Jack looked at the intruder and tried to hide his distaste.

'Wung Foo certainly fights if the contingency arises,' his owner replied. 'Don't you, my pretty?'

The Peke, which snuffed incessantly and wore a pink satin bow, seemed to blow out its cheeks and at the same time showed two rows of tiny, pointed teeth.

'Which of you is going to take him for a walkie? His little legs need stretching after the journey.'

Nobody spoke or moved. Mr Bagthorpe tried to catch the eyes of his offspring, and was making powerful grimaces. They all affected not to notice.

'*I* will!' he finally ground out. 'Give it here.'

He looked and felt extremely silly, as if he were leading a toy. Rosie giggled, and the minute he had left the room dashed out herself, presumably to fetch her camera.

'What time is breakfast?' inquired Great Aunt Lucy then. 'I am hungry.'

At this, Mrs Fosdyke made a choking sound. She had been staring at the arrival with ill-concealed curiosity and apprehension, while ostensibly polishing a brass plate.

'We thought in about half an hour,' interposed Mrs Bagthorpe swiftly, forestalling any comments Mrs Fosdyke might have to make. 'Tess, dear, take your Great Aunt up to her room, and be sure she has everything she wants.'

'It makes no matter what we *call* a meal,' Mrs Bagthorpe told an unco-operative Mrs Fosdyke, after the visitor had left the room. 'A rose by any other name would smell as sweet.'

'First time *I've* heard of pork chops and rhubarb dumplings for breakfast,' Mrs Fosdyke sniffed. 'Did you see all them watches pinned on her front? *None* of 'em the right time, as I could see. Broke, some of 'em looked. What kind of person goes round with dozens of broke watches pinned on their front?'

'It certainly looks extremely silly,' Grandma chipped in. She was already on her mettle. Great Aunt Lucy constituted a stronger threat than she supposed. 'As does that ridiculous hat. Some people, of course, will wear anything in order to draw attention to themselves.'

Jack wondered how any lady in her seventies, kitted out in a bee-keeping bonnet and veil in the total absence of hives, could make such a remark with a straight face.

'I may take up bee-keeping again.' It was as if Grandma had divined his thoughts.

'How lovely, Mother!' Mrs Bagthorpe enthused. 'We can then have delicious pure honey. Henry *will* be pleased.'

'I shall not do it to please Henry,' Grandma told her unnecessarily. 'I have immortal longings in me.'

At the time nobody could make much of this remark, unless to assume that Grandma, in the absence of an asp, intended to invite a Cleopatrian death by bee stings. Quite the reverse, however, was the case. Grandma had read some article about the beneficial effects of royal jelly, and now had the unbudgeable conviction that if one ate a sufficient number of queen bees, one would become immortal and quite rejuvenated. This prospect appealed strongly to her, especially following certain remarks made earlier to her by Daisy.

It was an unfortunate aspect of Daisy's new Intimations of Mortality Phase, that she was led to speculate on the

74

life-expectancy of everyone she now met. She tended to do this out loud.

'I don't fink you'll be alive very long, Grandma Bag,' she had said. 'You got a wrinkly face and blue hair and short legs.'

Grandma had reluctantly conceded the first two observations, but denied the last. She was very vain about her lower limbs, which were always set off in silk stockings and elegantly heeled shoes. It was, indeed, some time before the Bagthorpes cracked the mystery of short legs as a sign of impending demise. Daisy was taking into account only the portion of leg visible, and as elderly ladies tend to wear longer skirts than their younger counterparts, Daisy had concluded that shrinking of the legs was a sign of old age.

'If you *do* die,' Daisy had hastened to assure her, 'I'll have a lovely funeral for you, Grandma Bag. And I'll write a really long pome, and have about ten hymns, and everybody will cry.'

None of this was any real comfort to Grandma, who could see no joy in a funeral at which, in the nature of things, she would not be present.

'I shall keep bees,' she repeated. 'Henry shall go and procure hives immediately. I have forgotten most of what I knew, but the rest of you will surely help me.'

What Grandma really intended was that other people should look after the swarm, and she would consume the royal jelly and queen bees.

'Ah, Henry, there you are! I have decided that I shall —'

'Everybody out — quick!' ordered Mr Bagthorpe. He was panting hard. 'I let that accursed Peke off its lead and it's made off. Quick — the lot of you!'

Everyone moved, with the exception of Mrs Fosdyke and Grandma. The former made great play with basting the pork chops, the latter said coolly to anyone who might be listening:

'You had better make haste. That young man who murdered Thomas will be back soon, in his car, to bring my cat. We do not, I think, wish another victim.'

Mr Bagthorpe, who had meant to stay and regain his breath, groaned. He recognized the truth of this observation. He turned in his tracks, and lurched off out again, cursing.

Chapter Seven

The Bagthorpes scattered about the grounds, but were all within earshot when Mrs Fosdyke screamed. Some of them – notably Mr Bagthorpe and William – carried on their way regardless. The scream was a terrible one, but neither of them cared what was happening to Mrs Fosdyke, nor bothered to pretend he did. For this callousness they were rewarded by coming back eventually to find lunch almost over and Wung Foo curled up on a cushion by his owner. They had also missed a good scene.

What had happened was that Wung Foo had entered the kitchen trailing in his mouth the disinterred body of one of Daisy's corpses (the chicken, not the hamster). Judging by its multilated state, Wung Foo had been hiding under a bush somewhere chewing at it for some time, and was now bringing it in so that he could have another go at it later. It was not an appealing sight and was, moreover, distinctly malodorous. Aunt Lucy, astonishingly, was not the least perturbed by this.

'Darling Wung Foo is a hunter,' she informed everybody. 'How clever of him!'

'He can't be a hunter,' Rosie objected. 'The chicken was already dead. To be a hunter, you have to *kill* things.'

They all scowled at her, but she appeared not to notice.

'Wung Foo is a *humane* hunter,' Aunt Lucy told her severely. 'I will have no part in blood sports. What a curious breakfast menu you favour, Laura. I had rather expected kippers.'

'It is not breakfast-time,' Grandma told her. 'It is luncheon. Do you have difficulty in telling the time?'

'As I have already intimated, I do not recognize the existence of Time,' Aunt Lucy replied stiffly, 'and will thank you not to refer to it. It may be listening.'

'Did you enjoy your stay with Claud and Penelope?' interrupted Mrs Bagthorpe at this juncture. Grandma did not stand to benefit by Aunt Lucy's will, and was patently out to provoke her. This, however, could only put everyone else's bequests in jeopardy.

'I did not,' replied Aunt Lucy. 'I thought them excessively tedious. I thought I should have died of boredom. Moreover, I have the strong impression that the only reason I was invited there was that they hope to figure in my will.'

At this, something of a silence fell. The Bagthorpes studiously attended to their rhubarb dumplings. None of them wished to risk catching the old lady's eye. She was evidently a good deal more astute than anyone had given her credit for being.

'They will, of course, be disappointed,' she continued.

'They will?' prompted Mrs Bagthorpe, rather too hopefully to be in good taste. She thought that if Aunt Lucy then and there announced her intention of favouring Mr Bagthorpe's branch of the family, he would be instantly reassured, and would drop his Plan for Survival as abruptly as he had taken it up.

'Certainly they will,' Great Aunt Lucy told her. 'Everyone with expectations in that direction will be disappointed. As there is no such thing as Time, I shall outlive all these persons by decades – possibly by centuries.'

Nobody liked the sound of this, and Grandma least of all. Having only that day herself embarked on a scheme to ensure her own rejuvenation, she was much put out to find herself forestalled by a rival. She was casting swiftly about for a cutting rejoinder to Aunt Lucy's pronouncement, when Daisy offered *her* opinion of it.

'Silly griffin!' she exclaimed. (This was an expression

often used by Daisy, though nobody knew its source. Aunt Celia said it was a poetic metaphor.)

Aunt Lucy turned her attention toward the author of this remark just as Mr Bagthorpe, scarlet and breathless, appeared at the outer door.

'Silly griffin!' repeated Daisy. '*Everybody* dies, don't they, Grandma Bag? And then there's funerals. Even Grandma Bag's going to die one day, and she's my favourite of anybody. And you're older than her, *and* you've got shorter legs, *and* you're more wrinkly. You're really creased up and wrinkly. So you'll die first!'

Everyone sat appalled by this apparent destruction at a single blow of their hopes. Mr Bagthorpe clutched wordlessly at his hair. Grandma alone was undismayed – she was, indeed, enchanted.

'When you *do* die,' continued Daisy helpfully, 'jus' think, you might die while you're here! And if you do, I'll have a really nice funeral if you like and a lot of hymns and crying.'

Aunt Lucy looked far from taking up Daisy's offer (or at any rate, voluntarily). She had really led far too sheltered an existence to fit her for survival in such a household as the Bagthorpes'. Also, she was much used to being pandered to. The Bees in her Bonnet had always been kept slavishly supplied with nectar by those about her. (Even Aunt Penelope had conceded that Aunt Lucy's theories about time might be given some credence. 'A thousand ages in thy sight are but an evening gone,' she had mused.) It was years, then, since Great Aunt Lucy had been thus confronted with the stark truth. Never, possibly, had she been presented with a truth as stark as this.

The Bagthorpes waited with bated breath for her reaction. (The younger ones were torn between desiring the short-term benefits of her upping and leaving on the spot, and the longer-term of benefit of a sizeable bequest.)

Aunt Lucy sat gasping for quite a long time. She and Wung Foo were breathing in much the same way, Jack noted with interest.

In the end, Aunt Lucy disappointed nearly everyone by rising, still gasping, scooping Wung Foo under her arm, and making wordlessly for the door.

'Oh Lucy, dear!' protested Mrs Bagthorpe feebly, undecided whether to make after her, or let her go to her room alone and come to terms with the total disintegration of her world picture.

'I suppose we must give her time . . .' she murmured, not seeming aware of the irony of this remark.

'How very touchy she is,' remarked Grandma, hoping to trigger her son's repressed fury. 'I thought Daisy's offer most handsome. What a sweet and generous nature she has.'

Her strategy was successful. Within seconds Mr Bagthorpe was yelling, Daisy bawling, and the entire company into a fullscale furore. At its height Uncle Parker and Aunt Celia entered, having been unable to attract any attention by repeated ringing of the door bell. Aunt Celia immediately hurried to Daisy and clasped her tightly, wailing:

'Daisy, darling, why are you weeping?'

She repeated this query twice more, as if it were a refrain.

'Everybody's got to die, everybody has!' Daisy sobbed.

'Of course they have, my darling,' soothed her parent. 'Never send to know for whom the bell tolls – it tolls for thee!'

'Hell's *bells*!' yelled Mr Bagthorpe. 'Will you stop burbling about *bells*, for God's sake!'

Most people there heartily wished that bells were tolling, in earnest – for Daisy.

'Are you mad, Celia? That child has just pulled the kingpin from under every expectation I ever had. She has at a stroke reduced us all to eternal penury!'

He carried on yelling for some time in this vein, and talked a lot about lawsuits, and making claims for loss of expectations. Much of this was inaudible, however, because of strong competition for the floor from most others present. Aunt Celia was screaming about gold and dross and corruption, Uncle Parker was warning Mr Bagthorpe off his family, Grandma was talking about *her* will, Daisy bawling and Mrs Bagthorpe vainly trying to scream out advice from Stella Bright.

'It was like *The Fall of the House of Usher*,' Mrs Fosdyke later told her cronies in the Fiddler's Arms. 'Only worse. The row they was making, it's a wonder it didn't bring the roof in. There's no wonder that cat was out of its wits with fright.'

The cat referred to, the putative Thomas the Second, was not in fact introduced until the furore had been raging for a full ten minutes. No one had till then noticed that Uncle Parker was driving home some of his points by emphatic rappings of a large wicker basket, which could hardly have been reassuring to its occupant. It was Daisy, disengaging herself from her mother's protective embrace, whose eye first fell on it.

'The pussy!' she shrieked delightedly, her mood undergoing an abrupt change. 'That's the pussy!'

Everyone stopped shouting at once and all eyes were now riveted on the basket. In the silence there was a faint mewing and scratching. Mr Bagthorpe, his cup full, lurched off. His mouth was working, but nothing was coming out. A moment later the door of his study banged.

'Nasty Grook!' Daisy squealed after him. 'Daddy, Mummy, get the pussy out!'

The Bagthorpes watched numbly as Uncle Parker undid the catch. Daisy ran over and peered inside.

'Oooh, it's lovely!' she squeaked. '*I* want to give it to Grandma Bag!'

'Take care that it does not scratch or bite,' Aunt Celia told her anxiously.

The rest blanched. Daisy reached into the basket and scrabbled about before capturing its occupant. The kitten was bright ginger. Its dangling legs were tipped by claws unsheathed and sharp, its eyes were staring and wild. It was writhing frantically to escape Daisy's tight clutch.

She went over to Grandma.

'*Here* you are, Grandma Bag!' she cried, and plonked it directly in her lap.

'Oooeeech!' screamed Grandma, and the cat sprang in two bounds on to the dresser, where it arched and spat, fur stiffly on end. The Bagthorpes stared aghast, their worst fears apparently realized. Not so Daisy.

'Oh *Grandma*!' she squealed. 'You've frightened him! Poor little pussy. Look at his little legs all shaking!'

Grandma did not obey this instruction. She was currently more interested in her own limbs than those of the second Thomas. She was cautiously sliding up her frock to inspect the state of the damage. When she glimpsed the blood and the torn stockings, she let out a faint cry and dropped the hem.

'Mother, dear, are you all right?' inquired Mrs Bagthorpe anxiously.

'I should like some brandy,' Grandma replied faintly.

As Mrs Bagthorpe hurried off in search of this commodity, Grandma slowly and incredulously turned her gaze back towards her assailant. Now, the whole point about the original Thomas was that while he had spat at, scratched and bit indiscriminately and without provocation almost everyone within a considerable radius, he had made Grandma herself a notable exception to his attentions. Possibly, as Mr Bagthorpe pointed out, he had recognized in her a kindred spirit. He had actually lain in her lap and allowed her to stroke him and had even sometimes, she claimed, purred.

Grandma, clearly, had hoped and expected that the second Thomas would show exactly the same loathsome proclivities. Instead, here he was arched and spitting, his wild eyes fixed rivetingly on herself (it being she who had screamed). It was a case, as Mr Bagthorpe later pointed out with delight, of the biter bit.

Daisy then trotted forward.

'Poor pussy!' she said. 'You come to me.'

'Daisy!' moaned her mother protestingly.

Daisy's hands and face were already within scratching and biting range. The kitten, astonishingly, relaxed. Daisy's chubby fingers went under his chin, making little scrabbling movements. She then lifted him, unprotestingly, into her arms.

'He was frightened, poor little kit,' she told everyone. 'He likes me, don't you, little Tommy?'

This seemed indisputable. The Bagthorpes were disappointed by the unexpected development. Up to this juncture, it had seemed possible that Grandma would reject the animal out of hand. If, however, the cat liked Daisy, she would certainly be inclined to review the matter.

What happened next, therefore, was in the nature of a miracle. Great Aunt Lucy entered, leading Wung Foo.

Instantly Grandma and the kitten bristled. No one had expected to see the old lady reappear so soon after Daisy's ruthless estimate of her life expectancy. It had even seemed to them on the cards that she would never appear again.

'I think you had better take your animal out,' Grandma told Aunt Lucy, taking the offensive.

'And why is that?' inquired Aunt Lucy coolly.

'Because you would not wish, presumably, to see its eyes scratched out,' Grandma told her.

'Wung Foo is not afraid of cats,' replied the other. 'Perhaps you should remove *your* animal from the room.'

The Bagthorpes watched this interchange with keen attention. It seemed likely that what the pair of them were working up to was a kind of cockfight. The Bagthorpes were always interested in anything of a competitive nature, and were most of them already mentally improvising a system of scoring.

An impasse having now been reached, Grandma made a move to develop the situation.

'Put the cat down, Daisy,' she ordered. 'It cannot be comfortable being held so tightly.'

The Peke was straining at its leash and puffing and snorting. Jack felt that it more or less deserved to be attacked by Thomas the Second. Daisy, reluctantly, made to lower the kitten to the floor. At this, to the amazement of everyone, it began to whimper plaintively, and scrabble desperately to retain its hold on Daisy's pinafore.

'The animal is clearly terrified,' said Great Aunt Lucy smugly. 'Pray do not put it down, or it will be bitten. Why, might I ask,' she went on, addressing herself to Grandma, 'have you elected to have a cat of that colour? It is quite horrid.'

Jack held his breath.

'The animal does not belong to me,' replied Grandma, without turning a hair. 'It belongs to Daisy, and is, I think, a very attractive shade.'

There was a moment's silence while this appalling falsehood sank in, and then a moderate babble set up. Its main contributors were Aunt Celia, who had always turned down her daughter's impassioned pleas for a pussy on the grounds that cats clawed out people's eyes, and Daisy herself, made ecstatic by this generosity on Grandma's part. She loosed her hold on the kitten in order to embrace Grandma, Aunt Lucy let go of Wung Foo's lead, and next minute the recently averted confrontation was taking place. It was not strictly a confrontation, in that the last thing Thomas the Second appeared to desire was to confront Wung Foo. And had Daisy released her hold on her newly acquired pet, and allowed it to jump to safety, little damage would have been done.

In the event, a great deal of damage was done. Altogether three people were bitten – Daisy herself, with her stranglehold on the kitten, Aunt Celia, attempting to intervene, and Mr Bagthorpe, who had come striding in from his study to find out what was going on. Jack could not help feeling that it was very bad luck for his father to be bitten, and Mr Bagthorpe himself certainly thought so.

'There is no justice under the sun,' he declared, nursing his bleeding shin.

Grandma disagreed.

'You are always talking about poetic justice,' she told

him, 'and now you are experiencing it. You have no just cause for complaint.'

Mr Bagthorpe did a lot of very noisy complaining, both at the time, and afterwards. Despite the fact that it was Wung Foo who had bitten him, it was Uncle Parker, Daisy and Grandma to whom he allocated all blame. He acted as if it had been they who had bitten him.

All in all, it was a relief when Uncle Parker with his family, and Mrs Bagthorpe with her husband, drove off to the hospital in Aysham for tetanus shots.

Grandma was on the whole pleased with the way things had gone.

'That animal of yours is not so silly as it looks,' she told Great Aunt Lucy. 'Though it certainly showed lack of discrimination in biting darling Daisy, who has a natural empathy with all living creatures, great and small.'

This was news to the rest of the Bagthorpes. The only living – as opposed to dead – creatures with whom Daisy had in their experience demonstrated any affinity, was maggots.

'Shall we be waiting breakfast until Henry returns from the hospital?' inquired Aunt Lucy, ignoring this criticism. 'Darling Wung Foo and I are now ready for our kippers.'

Chapter Eight

To say that the situation at Unicorn House was now volatile would be badly to understate the matter. Almost every member of the household felt him or her self to be near the verge of breakdown – except, of course, Grandma and Daisy. Even Jack was beginning to feel edgy, mainly because of the strain of preventing a meeting between Zero and Wung Foo.

'It's undermining his confidence, being shut away half the time,' Jack thought. 'He's in solitary confinement, and that always affects people.'

He seemed to remember having read somewhere that people frequently lost all sense of identity during solitary confinement. This Zero could not afford to risk. His sense of identity was never strong at best. Jack tried to counter the effects of Zero's imprisonment by taking him for long walks during which he did a good deal of patting and praising. Mr Bagthorpe, however, soon put a stop to this.

'If you've got the energy to go twenty-mile hikes with that numskulled hound,' he told Jack, 'you've got the energy to dig. Get out there and dig.'

Mr Bagthorpe, once he had recovered from the shock and humiliation of being bitten by Wung Foo, had surveyed the courses open to him and decided that to forge ahead with his Master Plan for Survival was the only realistic one. He no longer entertained any real hopes of a bequest from Great Aunt Lucy.

'That accursed daughter of Russell's has put paid to that,' he said. He no longer bothered to be particularly polite to his visiting relation, now that there was nothing to be gained by this.

Astonishingly enough, considering that nobody in the household cared either for herself or her dog, Great Aunt Lucy stayed on. This pleased nobody. The pair of them caused great inconvenience. For one thing, Daisy had returned with her kitten, and evidently intended to prolong her stay, too, as long as possible (during which time, of course, there was the ever-present danger that the two animals might meet again, and there be some more biting).

'Grandma Bag and me's going to train Little Tommy up,' she told everybody.

No one was reassured by this intelligence. The two of them spent hours holed up in Grandma's room along with Little Tommy, and were almost certainly, Mr Bagthorpe said, brain-washing him, and using every technique at their disposal to ensure that he turned out a veritable hell-cat.

'Though at least it will be living, long term, with *that* lot,' he added, meaning Uncle Parker and Aunt Celia, 'and with any luck, will make their lives purgatory. *Mine*'s been purgatory long enough.'

His suspicions might well have been justified. Nobody knew for certain what the Unholy Alliance were up to during their training sessions, but Grandma, once Great Aunt Lucy was safely out of earshot, had certainly made no secret of her disgust at the showing put up by the kitten in its encounter with Wung Foo. It was this, indeed, that had prompted her to deny ownership. She wished for no association, she said, with anything so feeble.

'Milk and water creature!' she had exclaimed scornfully. 'Where is its spirit? Has it no fight? If only Thomas were still with me, in his great golden glory. No wishy-washy Pekingese would have been tolerated by him within his own house. He was an emperor among cats.'

The younger Bagthorpes felt that however intensive the

training the kitten was now receiving from Grandma and Daisy, it would be in no position to drive Great Aunt Lucy and Wung Foo out of the house in the foreseeable future. Nobody wished to wait this long.

'We must think of a way to clear them out ourselves,' William told his gloomy siblings. 'I am sick of being polite, and sick of having to keep closing doors to keep those two horrible animals apart. And I am sick to death of the eternal smell of kippers. She has had breakfast four times in the last twenty-four hours.'

'And I'm sick of always digging just to show her I've got determination,' Rosie said. 'Either that, or having to cook her horrible kippers. If she went, we wouldn't have to look as if we'd got strength of character.'

'The mere fact that she has been reduced to partaking of her breakfast at such ever-shortening intervals would seem to indicate that she feels herself to be, to some extent, threatened,' mused Tess. 'Perhaps we could turn this to our advantage. Evidently she is not currently coping with Time so well as she likes.'

'All that stuff Daisy said to her about legs and wrinkles couldn't have helped,' Jack said. 'Good old Daisy. And that funeral. Why don't we get Daisy to have a lot more funerals?'

There had been a lull in Daisy's undertaking activities since the advent of Little Tommy.

'That,' William told him, 'is not a bad idea.'

'But what about corpses?' objected Rosie. 'We haven't got any corpses.'

They sat and pondered this incontrovertible truth. Corpses were not, they realized, easily come by, even at Unicorn House.

'Where's she been getting her corpses up to now?' Jack asked. 'Uncle Park said she'd had about two dozen funerals last week. She can't have found two dozen corpses. She must've been burying other things as well.'

'That chicken...' William murmured thoughtfully. 'That was dead meat, all right...'

'Dead meat!' Jack was struck by a thought. 'Chops and things – out of the deep freeze!'

They considered this proposition. Whether or not Daisy would be moved to bury chops they were not certain. What they did know, was that once the supply of meat in the deep freeze was exhausted, Mr Bagthorpe had ruled that no more was to be purchased. Meat, therefore, was now at a premium. Thoughtful consideration was necessary. Things had to be weighed and balanced.

'What it amounts to,' William said, 'is whether a chop in the grave is worth two in a freezer.'

'Or vice versa,' Tess added.

'I think Daisy *could* bury chops,' Jack told the others. 'She's really dotty about burying things. I think we ought to egg her on.'

'A non-stop procession of funerals would certainly have a depressive effect on Aunt Lucy,' Tess said. 'What we could also do, is turn the conversation as much as possible to the subject of Time.'

This, too, was considered to be a sound proposition. Everyone undertook to do some rifling through books of poetry during spare moments, in search of apt quotations.

'And I'll have a quick scan through the hymn books,' William volunteered. 'Any thing about Time in them is usually pretty depressing.'

Jack and Rosie were deputed to catch Daisy during one of the rare moments when she was not in Grandma's room with Little Tommy, and make an effort to rekindle her apparently waning interest in funerals.

'Lay it on really thick,' William advised them. 'Say *you'll* go to the funerals. Tell her I've got a big bell, and'll toll it for her, if she likes. Tell her anything. And don't call the chops chops.'

'Why?' Rosie asked. 'What shall we call them, then?'

'Call them "poor little dead lambs",' he told her. 'Or piglets, as the case may be.'

'Will she be burying *sausages*?' Jack could not see even Daisy looking on these in the light of deceased piglets, and shedding tears over them.

'Pork *chops*, idiot!' William said. 'And while you're digging, keep your eyes open for anything dead. Or any odd bones.' (Daisy, he knew, had a powerful attraction toward skeletons, and had once tried to engineer William into becoming one himself.'

The younger Bagthorpes, then, scattered on their various missions, though these had to be dovetailed with their duties allotted by Mr Bagthorpe on his hell-bent career towards Self-Sufficiency. Currently, Tess was working on the salad section of the garden, Rosie acting as mate to William, who was converting the summer house to a hen house, and Jack just digging.

It was just after lunch (or supper, as Great Aunt Lucy preferred to call it) that Jack and Rosie managed to corner Daisy. They coaxed her into the sitting-room as she was on her way to fetch the kitten for an outing in the garden.

'I can't stop long,' she told them. 'Little Tommy mews when I'm not there.'

'The thing is, Daisy, we need your help,' Jack told her.

'What to do?' she asked. 'I'm not digging. I don't like digging. Except graves,' she added as an afterthought.

Rosie and Jack exchanged triumphant glances. Clearly Daisy was *not* out of her Intimations of Mortality Phase, and her undertaking urges were merely lying dormant.

'That's exactly what it is, Daisy,' Rosie told her. 'A grave. Poor little dead lamb.'

'Little dead lamb?' Daisy's eyes stretched. 'Where? Oh dear, poor little fing!'

Jack knew that the chop was going to prove something of an anticlimax for Daisy, who would be expecting something white and woolly, and accordingly chose his words carefully.

'It has been cut up, I'm afraid,' he told her.

'Oh *dear*!' squealed Daisy, aghast and enchanted at once. 'Oh, *poor* little fing! Oh, when shall we bury him?'

'As soon as you like,' Jack said. 'We'll come to the funeral as well, won't we, Rosie?'

'And Grandma Bag,' Daisy said happily. 'And will old Auntie Lucy come?'

'I shouldn't think so,' Rosie began, but Jack interrupted.

'That's a good idea. You ask her, Daisy.'

The more Great Aunt Lucy heard about Daisy's funerals, the better.

'I'll go and ask her.' Daisy trotted to the door. 'And I'll tell Grandma Bag. You go and get the poor dead lamb. I never buried a lamb before. I'll write him a lovely pome.'

From there on, things rapidly began to snowball. William had already abstracted several chops and other cuts of meat from the deep freeze, and these were defrosting in his room. He had enough potential corpses, he said, to keep Daisy going for days, if necessary.

'Though the sooner Aunt Lucy clears off the better,' he added. 'I'd give anything for a lamb chop with mint sauce.'

They all would. Meals, on Mr Bagthorpe's instructions, were becoming increasingly spartan. He too, it appeared, wished his elderly relative elsewhere.

Daisy invited Great Aunt Lucy to the funeral, but she strenuously declined.

'She said I mustn't *mention* poor dead fings.' Daisy told the rest indignantly as they assembled for the funeral of the chop. 'Silly old griffin!'

Daisy was, as had been anticipated, somewhat disappointed at the lack of resemblance of the chop to a real dead lamb, but soon perked up when she saw the increased number of mourners, and was informed that a bell would toll.

'And I'll take some photos,' Rosie promised.

William had selected a suitable spot for the interment, in full view of Great Aunt Lucy's window. She had gone up to her room for a doze because, she had informed them all at lunch, the full moon was now imminent. Mrs Fosdyke had a prolonged fit of choking when she heard this.

'I shall require some heavier curtains, Laura,' Great Aunt Lucy had continued. 'The present ones are quite inadequate. The rays of the moon will pass straight through them. I am already beginning to be affected by them.'

Mrs Bagthorpe had looked quite desperate at this, and Jack longed to tell her that her fears were groundless, because the old lady would almost certainly have left before the full moon.

Aunt Lucy was wakened, as had been intended, by the loud tolling of William's bell, and Jack, glancing up, saw her inadequate curtains move, and caught a glimpse of her face.

The funeral went swimmingly. Daisy, once she had accepted the fact that her corpse was dismembered, acted as bereaved as she ever had. A further funeral took place several hours later, and she wept at that, too.

'Poor dead piglet, poor dead piglet!' she sobbed as the pork chop was laid in its shallow grave. 'Dusters to dusters, ashes to ashes!'

The younger Bagthorpes themselves found that they, too, were enjoying the proceedings, though they sometimes had difficulty in disguising their giggles as sobs, and Tess was in fact reproved for this on one occasion.

'You *never* laugh at funerals,' Daisy told her severely. 'You *cry*. Jus' try to fink of the poor dead lamb. How would *you* like to be a poor dead lamb?'

A relentless procession of chops, then, made their way

to the grave, and a curious assortment of headstones sprang up in the part of the garden designated as the graveyard. Daisy was running out of things large enough for her to write her epitaphs on, so had now adopted the policy of selecting articles for their ornamental value, and then attaching her poems on sheets of paper either sellotaped or pinned on. There was a cross formed by a ruler and silver spoon taped together, a brass candlestick, a pair of cast iron Punch and Judy doorstops and a large Staffordshire figure which, Daisy said, reminded her of an angel.

She was increasingly exercised in the composition of suitable epitaphs, because all her corpses at present fell into only two categories.

'I'm getting *bored* writing pomes jus' about lambs and piglets,' she said, as she attached her latest composition to Mr Bagthorpe's shooting stick. 'I wish I could bury something different. For ever and ever amen.'

The epitaph read:

> All the lams are dying
> All the lams are ded
> Evryone is crying
> Cos the lams has gone to bed.
> Forever and evver.
> 1629–1842

This seemed to Jack to have a more than usually final ring to it. Daisy's boredom threshold was notoriously low. He intensified his search for something more out of the way for her to work on. In the meantime, William told her that one of the chops was a cow, and another a giraffe, it being unlikely that Daisy would see through this fraud.

The other prong of the campaign to drive Great Aunt Lucy away was also going extremely well. When the

94

younger Bagthorpes were hatching up their scheme to steer conversation whenever possible to the subject of Time, they were not aware that Grandma had privately decided on exactly the same line of action herself. She had already a considerable repertoire of gloomy quotes that she would come up with when she was feeling low.

> Like as the waves make towards the pebbled shore
> So do our minutes hasten to their end

was one of her favourites, and she was also fond of telling everybody:

> Time, like an ever-rolling stream,
> Bears all its sons away.

Mealtimes, then, became extremely morbid occasions, what with the insipidity of the menus, most people wearing black because of the imminence of yet another funeral, and the lugubrious nature of the conversation. When even Rosie started coming out with things like:

> But at my back I always hear
> *Time's* wingèd chariot hurrying near

and

> Gather ye rosebuds while ye may,
> Old *Time* is still a-flying,

with particular emphasis on the word Time, Mr Bagthorpe cottoned on to what was happening. He did nothing to prevent it, however, and even stopped his wife from doing so.

'It'll do 'em good, ferreting round for all those quotations,' he told her. 'They have read more Shakespeare in the last two days than in the rest of their lives put together. They are rounding off their education. It is an ill wind, Laura — try to look at it like that.'

'I do think it is all rather unfair on the poor old lady,' she told him.

'Bilge,' returned Mr Bagthorpe. 'Poor nothing. If she's got a Bee in her Bonnet about Time, it's our duty to smoke it out, not pander to it.'

When Mrs Bagthorpe pointed out that a reluctance to accept the idea of mortality was not strictly a Bee in the Bonnet, but a fairly common human frailty, he replied that he did not agree. No life could be properly lived except in the full consciousness of eventual death, he said, and furthermore, some people even welcomed the prospect, as he did himself, at times.

'And if eating kippers at all the hours God sends is not a Bee in the Bonnet, you tell me what is,' he said. 'William had better get on to that Anonymous fellow from Grimsby and get him to catch further supplies. The North Sea will soon be bled dry of kippers.'

'But she may genuinely *believe* there is no such thing as Time,' Mrs Bagthorpe persisted. 'I really think she does. I think we should give her the benefit of the doubt.'

Mr Bagthorpe was not in the habit of giving anyone the benefit of the doubt, and he was not about to start now.

'If she genuinely does not believe in Time,' he replied, 'then the only logical thing for her to do is to clear off to where there *isn't* any — namely, eternity.'

Great Aunt Lucy was, in fact, about to clear off. She shuffled, however, not off this mortal coil, but off out of the Bagthorpe household and into hospital. This calamity was brought about entirely by herself, and nobody, Mrs Bagthorpe said, was likely to be cut out of her will on account of it.

'If, indeed, any of us still figure in it,' she added worriedly. 'I do think you have all tormented the old lady dreadfully.'

'Rubbish, Laura,' Grandma told her with asperity. 'She enjoyed every moment of her stay. She aggravated every one of us, and enjoyed doing so. I could tell.'

She probably could. When it came to aggravating people, Grandma could teach most people a few things – and certainly Great Aunt Lucy, who was not even in the same league.

Chapter Nine

The immediate cause of Great Aunt Lucy's being admitted to the Nightingale Ward of Aysham General Hospital was a broken leg, but the real reason, she later claimed, was the quality of the lining of the curtains in her room. This did not at once emerge, as the old lady was understandably shocked and rambling after her injury, but when the true facts came to light, Mrs Bagthorpe was quite distraught. Her deep breathing failed. She went, temporarily, into being a failed Stella Bright.

'I should have *listened*!' she wailed, to an audience more fascinated by her derangement than by what she was actually saying. 'She *knew* that the rays of the moon were affecting her, and I dismissed it all as idle superstition!'

'It *was* idle superstition,' her husband told her. 'Pull yourself together, Laura. If the sanity of mankind hinged upon the utilization of super-quality curtain linings, the race would have become extinct at the palaeolithic era. No cave, so far as I know, made use of such a product.'

'They used animal hides,' Rosie told him. 'Animal hides are a lot thicker than *any* curtain, even velvet.'

'Be quiet,' he told her, irritated by the realization that a pertinent point had been made. 'Your mother is in no mood for that kind of trivial talk. Lucy had an outsized Bee in her Bonnet, and is paying the price. We must all hope that she will emerge from the experience a little older and wiser.'

'Older, anyway,' William put in, 'though she'll never admit it.'

The amazing thing was that Mr Bagthorpe's hopes were eventually realized. Great Aunt Lucy did emerge (though not for three weeks) considerably wiser. She emerged, in fact, converted to a belief in Time. What brought about this miraculous change was not breaking her leg, *per se*, but her stay in hospital. The manner of her accident had indisputably been brought about by her strenuous belief in the sinister influence of the moon's rays. She had been roaming about the house at dead of night in search of kippers, in order to convince both Time and the moon that it was breakfast-time, when she had tripped against a sack of mushrooms, and fallen. (Normally, bags of mushrooms would not have been lying around on the landing, but Mr Bagthorpe had heard that a great saving could be made by raising these fungi in a large bag of suitably compounded compost, and had accordingly invested in one.)

The rest of the household were woken by Aunt Lucy's screams and the barking of Wung Foo. They emerged from their rooms bleary-eyed and bad-tempered, to find out what was going on. When they did find out, sympathy for Aunt Lucy was scant.

'Why, Lucy, in the name of all that is wonderful, did you not switch on the *light*?' demanded Mr Bagthorpe.

The patient was in no mood for cross-examination, though one was inevitably to take place later, in hospital, to the intense interest of the rest of the ward. It later transpired, however, that not turning on lights was part of her strategy to fool Time. She maintained that if lights were turned on, then Time would *know* it was night, and she had accordingly tried to sneak past Time with a small torch. This had failed to pick out the bag of mushrooms.

Great Aunt Lucy had already established a minor reputation for eccentricity by the time the Bagthorpes went to visit her the following day (though the hospital was not yet acquainted with the full range of Bees in her Bonnet). The ward sister had been able to make little of Aunt

Lucy's description of how the accident occurred. She asked the Bagthorpes to give her the real facts.

'People simply do not fall over sacks of mushrooms on landings in the middle of the night,' she said.

'At our place they do,' Mr Bagthorpe told her. 'How long is she going to be in here?'

'It is for the doctors to say, of course,' replied the sister. 'But I should imagine for several weeks – especially at her age. And perhaps you could tell me, incidentally, what her age is? She doesn't appear to know, and became quite agitated when we pressed her.'

'She would,' Mr Bagthorpe told her. 'If you've got her for a month, you'll find out how agitated she gets, all right. And for all our sakes, try to get her sorted out, will you? She's eighty-seven.'

'May we see her now?' inquired Mrs Bagthorpe.

'There is rather a large number of you,' the sister said dubiously.

'Look,' said Mr Bagthorpe, 'we do not have the time, and nor can we afford the petrol, to pay daily visits here for the next few weeks. We are trying to Survive. We will take our full quota of visiting time for the week now, please.'

With this he marched past her and the rest of the family trailed after him. Great Aunt Lucy was halfway down the ward, propped up on pillows and with a hooped cage over her legs. Nobody else had visitors (it was not, in fact, visiting time, simply a time convenient to Mr Bagthorpe) and all eyes followed the procession with interest.

'It's not visiting time, is it?' asked the woman in the next bed to Aunt Lucy.

'There is no such thing as Time,' Aunt Lucy told her coldly. 'Kindly do not refer to it again in my presence. Ah, there you are, Henry and Laura! Why did you put a sack of mushrooms on the landing where I was almost certain to fall over it?'

'If the light had been switched on, you would have seen it,' Henry told her. 'And you should have been in bed, asleep, the same as anybody else, not roving abroad in search of kippers.'

'It was breakfast-time,' Aunt Lucy asserted obstinately. 'You do not switch on lights at breakfast-time.'

The listeners in the surrounding beds, having all observed Great Aunt Lucy's entry into the ward at two a.m., raised eyebrows at one another. They had also witnessed her refusal of breakfast.

'I have no wish for a poached egg,' she had informed a bewildered orderly. 'I am not in the habit of consuming poached eggs at lunch-time. I should like a lamb chop please, lightly grilled, and mint sauce.'

In the end, the orderly had fetched the ward sister, who gave it as her opinion that Aunt Lucy was still under the effect of the anaesthetic.

'She will be right as rain by lunch-time,' she forecast optimistically.

Daisy, who had never been in hospital (except as an outpatient), had pleaded to be brought along too. Her reasons for this had nothing to do with a wish to comfort her Great Aunt, and everything to do with her current preoccupation with mortality.

'We might even see some *skelingtons*,' she confided hopefully to Rosie. 'And there'll be people all cut up.'

She was very interested in the ward, and trotted up and down it. The inmates, enchanted by her cherubic appearance, and unaware that Daisy was in search of a skelington or, failing that, a corpse, made much of her. Before long Daisy was relaying to a fascinated audience details of life as lived by the Bagthorpes.

'I been having funerals,' she told them. 'Every day. And I been burying poor little dead lambs and giraffes. And I know all the proper words to say, and I say "dusters to dusters and ashes to ashes for ever and ever amen".

And Grandma Bag helps me, but she's not here because she don't like old Auntie Lucy. She thinks she's a nasty Grook.'

Meanwhile, at Aunt Lucy's bedside, a furore was gradually gathering momentum, and the patients were torn between listening to that and hearing more from Daisy. The nurses began to hover anxiously, wondering whether or not to put the Bagthorpes out, and if so, how on earth to set about this.

Mr Bagthorpe was beginning to shout. The subject of Wung Foo's accommodation during his owner's stay in hospital had been broached. It was she herself who brought it up.

'Where is darling Wung Foo?' she inquired. 'I hope that you have remembered to bring his little bowl?'

'But, Lucy dear, one cannot keep a dog in hospital,' Mrs Bagthorpe said.

'Why not?' she demanded. 'There seem to me to be a good number of people here who would be able to exercise him for me. The rest of the time he can stay on my bed.'

'We will take every care of him,' Mrs Bagthorpe promised.

'We will what?' It was at this point that Mr Bagthorpe began to run out of control. 'We already have in the house the most numb-brained, non-productive hound that ever went on four legs, but at least it does not feed on kippers at all hours of the day and night, and nor has it, to date, bit. That Peke of yours bit me, Lucy, and nobody can go around expecting hands that get bitten to go around feeding the mouth that bit them.'

He was becoming incoherent. Also, of course, it was not his hand that had been bitten, but his shin. His wife was not herself anxious to have custody of Wung Foo for any length of time. If he bit Mrs Fosdyke, she would leave for ever.

Mrs Fosdyke was already becoming restive about the new dietary arrangements, and had made no effort to conceal her satisfaction on hearing that Great Aunt Lucy was no longer at Unicorn House.

'Hospital's where she belongs, leg broke or not,' she had declared. 'She ain't fit to be loose. Weeks it'll be before we get that horrible smell of kippers out of the furnishings. I thought fish bones was meant to *make* brains, not turn 'em.'

She had soliloquised thus at some length, though nobody, of course, paid any attention, because they were all arguing with their mouths full, as was customary at Bagthorpe mealtimes.

Mrs Bagthorpe now, however, timidly put in her own oar.

'I think, Lucy dear, that Wung Foo will be much happier in proper kennels,' she said diplomatically. 'Pekingese are such delicate creatures, and need much sensitive handling.'

'Which will *not* be forthcoming at our place,' Mr Bagthorpe supplied unnecessarily. 'If it stopped there, it'd probably have a nervous breakdown. I certainly should. It will go to the kennels, and you, Lucy, will foot the bill.'

Aunt Lucy was not going to give in this easily, and was about to embark on a thoroughgoing row when a diversion occurred in the shape of an elderly lady at the far end of the ward rising from her pillows, waving her arms wildly, and screaming for a nurse.

'Take her away!' she screeched, meaning, apparently Daisy. 'I won't listen, I won't!'

She covered her ears with her hands, and a contingent of nurses moved rapidly down to her end of the ward.

'What is the matter?' they asked. 'What has she done?'

What Daisy had been doing soon became clear. Abandoning with disappointment her fruitless search for skelingtons and corpses, she had turned her attention to the patients themselves. Some of them, she thought hopefully, might become corpses quite soon, and she could put in an offer for the undertaking.

She had therefore been systematically working down the row of beds, making a critical appraisal of the life expectancy of their occupants. She was to some extent handicapped in this by being unable to see the length of their lower limbs, and was accordingly asking each lady, 'Is your legs long or short?' before making her diagnoses.

The ladies in the ward had been held in a state of hypnotized fascination, until one of their number had started screaming. The sort of things Daisy was saying no one present (and many of them were mothers and grandmothers) had ever heard from the lips of one so young. And they had no idea, of course, of her background, or that she was currently in a Phase of Intimations of Mortality. She was saying things like,

'Ooooh, look at *your* hair! It's all grey. And you've got a lot of wrinkles as well, specially on your neck. I fink you might die quite soon, really soon. Is your legs long or short?'

She made her speculations in so matter-of-fact a way that her subjects actually felt that she might know something about the matter, and those among them with grey hair and wrinkles were quite frightened.

When Daisy's part in the screaming episode was established, she in turn became extremely unhappy, and sobbed bitterly. Aunt Celia was not there to protect her, and Mr Bagthorpe, abandoning his row with Great Aunt Lucy, pitched into her on a scale never before known. Jack found himself feeling sorry for her. He did not pretend to understand the way Daisy's mind worked, he thought it possible that nobody ever would understand this, but he felt certain that however cataclysmic the effect she so often had on those about her, it was quite unintentional. Daisy did not really have any vice in her, it was just that she liked experimenting — with fire and water, for instance — and that she became bored when she was not occupied. Jack had been impressed by the way Daisy had been shedding real tears over her recent victims (including the chops). He thought this showed an essential softness of heart for which people were not apt to give her credit — with the exception of Rosie, who herself deputized for Aunt Celia by attacking Mr Bagthorpe.

'You're a nasty Grook, just like Daisy says!' she shrieked at him. 'You don't care tuppence when things die and get buried! Daisy's really sweet the way she sobs and cries and has funerals and writes on their tombstones! If you don't look out, I shan't cry when *you're* dead!'

All this bandying about of words like tombstones and funerals, and at a pitch more suited to a music hall than a hospital ward, was becoming too much. One of the younger nurses panicked and telephoned the matron. She had heard that this august person was a battleaxe when roused, and thought that she, if anybody, would be able to quieten and evict the Bagthorpes.

She was mistaken about this, because Mr Bagthorpe knew nothing of hospital hierarchies, and did not at first even know that she *was* the matron. He thought she was a stout, elderly nurse in a different uniform from the rest. Even when he had been made to understand who she was, matters were improved for nobody but Daisy, from whom he immediately turned his attention to pitch into the matron instead.

Mr Bagthorpe detested bureaucracy and authority in any form, even at the best of times, and of course believed that he was in his present plight as a direct result of the activities of these nebulous enemies. So far he had not confronted anybody, even his bank manager, about this, and the luckless matron made a convenient whipping boy.

'I would not at this moment be in the throes of a desperate fight for Survival,' he told this bewildered lady, 'if it were not for the System. You are part of the System. You do not run this hospital – *I* do. You, madam, are a servant of the State. I am for ever paying out vast sums of money left and right in taxation for the maintenance of this kind of benighted institution.'

Mr Bagthorpe often did not know when he was mistiming his tirades. A ward full of semi-hysterical patients and frantic nurses do not wish for an exposition on taxation. They wish for order to be restored, for peace and quiet.

The scene ended in a way that was less than dignified. The same resourceful nurse who had called the matron reassessed the situation and sent for two porters. Their burly and belligerent appearance caused Mr Bagthorpe's tirade to tail off in mid-sentence.

'I am leaving,' he announced, 'and I shall not be back. You, Lucy, should try to take advantage of the next few weeks to get your ideas sorted out. Put your house in order.'

He stamped out followed by the rest of the Bagthorpes and all eyes in the ward. Most of the patients were left feeling distinctly limp after this visit, and Mrs Fosdyke later received a first-hand account of it from one of her cronies, Mrs Pye, who was in there to have some ingrowing toenails removed. She had been one of the luckless ladies with grey hair and wrinkles, and Daisy had firmly placed her in the category of being in early need of burial. Mrs Pye was much upset by this, despite repeated assurances from the sister and nurses that people do not die of ingrowing toenails.

'Them Bagthorpes you work for certainly is a bunch of lunatics,' she told Mrs Fosdyke after her discharge. 'Them nurses was dishing out tranquillizers like sweets. You never in your life could imagine the racketing they set up in that ward.'

Mrs Fosdyke denied this. She could imagine it, she said, clearly. Only that day Mrs Fosdyke had received further indications of the seriousness of the Scheme for Survival and was considering, not for the first time, giving her notice.

'You never heard such mad twaddle in your life,' she told Mrs Pye. 'That beautiful summer house – there's all the deck-chairs and parasols stuck in my outhouse, and wire netting all over everywhere. And the food they're eating you'd never believe. It's all right for them that's been bankrupted, and *got* to Survive, but what about them that hasn't?'

Her own health, she maintained, was probably being damaged (she took a large number of her meals at Unicorn House) by all the lettuce and rhubarb and beetroot. She had a cousin, Kitty, who had died of an overdose of vitamings, she said, and she had no wish to go the same way herself.

Chapter Ten

The Bagthorpes now really began to feel that they were, as Mr Bagthorpe maintained, ranged up against the whole world. More accurately, they felt that the whole world was ranged up against *them*. They were used to a moderate degree of unpopularity. People who are brilliant and, what is worse, constantly boast about this, seldom attract warm and friendly feelings from other people. But the Bagthorpes did, however surprisingly, have several friends, with the exception of Mr Bagthorpe, who had none. He was accordingly less affected by this chilling off in relationships.

Anyone friendly with the Bagthorpes knew, naturally, that they were not quite as others. Some people found them quite entertaining, and liked hearing about their fires and floods, and so forth. But the friendship of these people was now being tested. A lot of the young Bagthorpes' friends were accustomed to coming up to Unicorn House for meals. They were always well worth coming for. People would walk or cycle for miles to catch a slice of Mrs Fosdyke's apricot cream gateau, or one of her stuffed eggs. Having partaken of these, they would then circulate rhapsodic descriptions of the experience to acquaintances, and regular visitors were therefore more in the nature of an unofficial Gourmet Society than bona fide lovers and admirers of the Bagthorpes themselves.

It was, then, the falling off of standards of cuisine, rather than the Bagthorpes' Plan for Survival *per se* that was responsible for the rapid decline in their social life. Nobody, as William bitterly pointed out (his latest girl friend having become cool) is going to walk even fifty yards for lukewarm beetroot salad, followed by gooseberry fool made with half milk and half water. The Bagthorpes were themselves beginning to lose their appetites, and most of them were losing weight.

'*I* shall be bankrupt soon!' wailed Rosie. (Her savings were being rapidly depleted by frequent visits to the village shop for supplementary rations.) 'It's not fair! Children aren't supposed to have to buy their own food. Their fathers are supposed to feed them. I bet there's a law against it!'

The idea of taking legal action against Mr Bagthorpe was actually seriously considered. The younger Bagthorpes were quite prepared to do this in principle. There was, however, one insurmountable deterrent. The Bagthorpes had had a good deal of adverse publicity during the preceding year, some of it reaching the national press and television networks. A court case brought against a father by his own offspring would only invite further unwelcome headlines.

'And just think how that ghastly Luke and Esther'd gloat,' said Rosie glumly. 'The only reason they're jealous of us is because we've got Fozzy's cooking, and they only have lettuce and nuts. If they knew *we* get lettuce as well, think how they'd *smirk*!'

The truth of this was patent and incontrovertible, and the idea of instigating litigation against their father was reluctantly abandoned. The young Bagthorpes, however, were not of the stuff of which martyrs are made. They did not suffer setbacks with stoicism. If circumstances did not suit them, they made all-out efforts to change them. If there was no way Mr Bagthorpe could be coaxed or coerced out of his current obsession, then their only course, they decided, was to enter into it equally wholeheartedly themselves.

'There is no question of becoming immortal,' Tess wisely pointed out, 'if one is not even able to achieve Survival.'

They accordingly dropped their frenzied pursuit of immortality, and channelled all their considerable energies into Survival. By and large they were temporarily united in this. Unfortunately, however, there very soon occurred a major rift as a result of certain events later in the day of the Bagthorpes' visit to hospital.

Daisy, upset by her unsympathetic treatment there, set about consoling herself by holding another couple of funerals on her return. Nobody but Rosie and Grandma was interested in assisting her in these, however, because now that Great Aunt Lucy was out of the way, everybody else had lost their motivation. Only William, surprisingly, complied.

'There's still a couple of lamb chops left,' he said. 'Might as well tell her they're a lion cub and a panda, and let her bury 'em. It'll keep her out of the way.'

The others did not care one way or the other, and said she could bury them if she liked, but they wanted no part in the funeral arrangements. Nobody even saw the processions, but the ceremonies had evidently been a great success.

'I never buried a baby lion before,' Daisy told everybody happily at tea-time. 'And lion rhymes with dying, so the pome was easy.' (Daisy made extensive use of poetic licence. Jack later saw the tombstone of the purported panda, and it read: Here ther is a pore ded panda, pekked to deth by goosy ganda.)

Nobody encouraged this line of conversation, and the matter of the funerals was dropped until the following morning, when it was raised again with a vengeance. Daisy, it appeared, did not just bury her remains and then forget them. She visited their graves to inspect them and sometimes change the flowers. And on this particular occasion she went further. Although she so frequently made use of the phrase 'dusters to dusters and ashes to ashes', she had recently been much exercised by the question of whether her corpses actually *were* metamorphosed in this way, and if so, how long it took. Were the assortment of toffee tins and chocolate boxes used as coffins and recently interred, actually now containing dusters and ashes, she wondered? Her curiosity had reached such a pitch that, being Daisy, she had no alternative but to satisfy it. She had decided to exhume one of yesterday's fatalities first, and then, if the results were disappointing, go back to an earlier corpse, Rosie's hamster, and take a look at that. In the event, her experiment was short-lived.

Daisy was an incurably early riser, and the whole household was therefore woken by her shrieks. She ran first, naturally, to Grandma's room, and most other people assembled there to see what was happening. No one but Rosie, and possibly Mrs Bagthorpe, much cared what had happened to Daisy. They simply, being Bagthorpes, found a furore, of whatever kind, irresistible.

It was some time before Grandma, still half awake and befuddled, could elicit from her protégée what was causing her present distress. Daisy was sobbing uncontrollably, and only odd words and phrases were intelligible.

'Gone for ever and ever amen!' she wailed. And 'Nuffing, now, not even dusters and ashes and anyfing! Poor fings, poor fings!'

The baffled Bagthorpes little by little pieced together some kind of picture. The gist of what was being said seemed, incredibly, to be that some of Daisy's most recent victims had been exhumed during the night.

'The child is raving,' said Mr Bagthorpe decisively. 'That blasted Peke is fifteen miles away by now, thank God.'

'Hush!' cried Grandma. 'Daisy is distressed beyond all measure!'

'We're *all* distressed beyond all measure,' he told her unrepentantly, 'as, indeed, we can count upon being, whenever that unholy infant is in the vicinity. We are to take it, then, that there is a grave-robber at large?'

'Certainly there is,' replied Grandma. 'Daisy's word is her bond. I shall put on my wrap and go instantly to investigate.'

'There is no need for that Mother,' interposed Mrs Bagthorpe. 'The dew may have been quite heavy. Jack will go, won't you, dear?'

Jack went. He stared in amazement at the soil-speckled toffee tin that had held the remains of the fraudulent lion cub. It was empty.

'She could've forgotten to put the chop in,' he thought, though without conviction. Daisy was nothing if not thorough. Jack seemed to remember that Daisy was enclosing her chops in plastic bags, and *then* placing them in their various coffins. He also, now he came to think of it, seemed to remember that this had been at William's suggestion. William, indeed, had been uncharacteristically helpful over the whole business of chop-burying, especially considering his views about Daisy, which were frequently aired, and unflattering to a degree.

'It will be more hygienic, Daisy,' he had said on this occasion, obligingly proffering a polythene bag.

'Oh, fank you, William!' Daisy had squealed. 'What's hygienic?'

'It's something everybody needs to be,' he told her, 'alive or dead.'

Daisy, while by no means a conformist, nor even particularly hygienic, had been happy to observe this formality. It had been an extra little ritual for her to enjoy, putting the chops carefully into their polythene bags before enclosing them in their tins and boxes.

On impulse, Jack stirred with his foot the loose soil of the adjacent grave, that of the panda. He could see the pattern of the tin lid showing through (Daisy's graves were all very shallow). He hesitated. It *did* seem sacrilege, of a sort.

'It's only a *chop*,' he told himself.

He knelt and scrabbled with his fingers and easily lifted out the tin. He opened it. It was empty. He set off back for the house still carrying it. It would be evidence, he thought, that Daisy was telling the truth, if nothing else. Though he thought he had now put two and two together.

He had. When the true story emerged it was like, as Mr Bagthorpe observed, something straight out of Dracula.

'We are embarked on a full-scale tilt into the macabre,' he declared, 'and I shudder to think how this family might end up. What in the name of the devil have we spawned?'

'Only *William*,' Rosie protested. 'Greedy thing!'

'It was not greed,' corrected her father. 'It was nothing like so simple as that. It was sheer, blind, carnivorous craving. It was a primitive blood lust.'

Jack thought Mr Bagthorpe was exaggerating, in that William had not killed the chops, merely eaten them. He guessed, rightly, that his father was chagrined that he had not thought of this idea first.

'He consumed them at midnight,' Mr Bagthorpe continued, 'at dead of night he conducted this grisly post mortem. I suspect that he did not even use a knife and fork. I suspect that he held them in his fingers and tore at the flesh. Did you, by any chance, devour them raw?'

'I grilled them,' William replied. 'And I had mint sauce with the lamb ones. They're the best thing I've had for days. I ate every single chop she buried, if you want to know.'

He was not at all repentant, and refused to allow that there was anything Satanic, or even macabre, about his actions.

'The chops had merely been laid in the cool earth rather than a fridge,' he said, 'as they would have been before fridges were invented. You are just jealous because you didn't think of it yourselves.'

They were, of course, almost to a man, with the exception of Mrs Bagthorpe, Daisy, and Grandma, the latter secure in her possession of a Fortnum and Mason hamper. Rosie would dearly have liked a grilled chop, but certainly not at the expense of hurting Daisy's feelings.

'Poor little Daisy – you never thought of *her*!' she shrieked at William.

'I did not,' he assented. 'I never gave her a second's thought. I put the graves back how they were, and if she hadn't gone poking around she'd never have known. It's *her* that's morbid.'

'It's not! It's not! She cried and cried and cried. She thinks that all the things she's buried have vanished into thin air for ever and ever and now she's really upset!'

'What she was probably looking for,' William continued, 'was maggots.'

'She wasn't then! She thinks things turn to dusters and ashes, and I think it's really sweet! And –'

'I think we are going round in circles,' Mr Bagthorpe

intervened. 'You know, don't you' – addressing himself to William –'that your grandmother is talking of cutting you out of her will? I should have thought that a high price to pay for a couple of clandestine chops.'

'And Daisy's going to train Little Tommy up to scratch you,' Rosie put in, '*and* bite you. And it'll serve you right!'

Grandma and Daisy had certainly been holed up in the former's room once the initial furore died down. Grandma had been extremely scathing prior to her withdrawal.

'You have betrayed at a stroke the innocent dreams of a little child,' she told William. 'That is the eighth, and the most heinous, of the Seven Deadly Sins. You should wear sack-cloth and ashes for the rest of your days.'

Her Old Testament line and the unfortunate reference to ashes made no impression at all on William, and served only to heighten Daisy's hysteria.

'I fought fings turned to dusters and ashes,' she sobbed. 'And now they don't, and I'm not having funerals any more. I hate funerals!'

'Of course you do not, dear child,' Grandma told her. 'And of *course* things turn to dusters and ashes, if they are not interfered with. We shall hold many more lovely funerals, and put this whole sordid business behind us.'

'I'm going to tell Arry Awk!' Daisy wailed, unsoothed.

At this all present, including Grandma, stiffened. If the exhumation of the chops had brought about the resurrection of Arry Awk, who had been conspicuous by his absence of late, then things were taking a more dangerous turn. He was, they well knew, the most malignant and slippery member of the Unholy Alliance. Despite his invisibility to the eyes of anyone but Daisy, he certainly knew how to make his presence felt. He also enabled Daisy and Grandma to perpetrate whatever atrocities they chose, and then disclaim all responsibility by blaming them all on the tireless Arry Awk.

'Arry Awk is the Archetypal Can-carrier of all time,' Mr Bagthorpe would declare. 'I should know. I am one myself.'

'If Arry Awk is again among us,' he now said, 'we must look to ourselves. We are already beset with cannibalism (meaning, presumably, William) and saboteurs (meaning Daisy and Grandma). Now we have a hell-raising entity who will strike at any time, from all sides. Mayhem will break loose.'

A profound silence followed this statement. It was broken by the rattling of the doorknob that heralded the arrival of Mrs Fosdyke. The Bagthorpes tried to rally themselves into some kind of appearance of normality, but failed signally.

'Morning!' Mrs Fosdyke kept shooting suspicious looks at them as she whipped about donning her overall and fur-edged slippers. The Bagthorpes, in their strenuous effort to look normal, in fact appeared less so than usual.

Grandma rose.

'Come, Daisy,' she said. 'We will leave others to explain to Mrs Fosdyke the grisly proceedings of the past few days. She may wish to consider seriously whether or not she wishes to be attached to such a household.'

Having made this intentionally inflammatory speech she withdrew, taking Daisy with her.

'What's been going on, then?' demanded Mrs Fosdyke flatly.

'Nothing,' replied the young Bagthorpes in unison. Unlovable as Mrs Fosdyke was, she could at least do more with rhubarb and beetroot than any of themselves. She had even produced a moderately acceptable soup with the latter.

'What's on for today, then?' Mrs Fosdyke asked. 'It's never lettuce and onions again?'

'I had rather thought a salad at lunch,' Mrs Bagthorpe

said apologetically. 'And then this evening, I thought an omelette?'

'An omelette?' Rosie echoed. '*One* omelette, between us all?'

'Don't be an idiot,' William told her. 'Have you forgotten? The hens are coming today.'

'My chickens!' she exclaimed joyously. 'Hurrah! I'm going to give them all names, and call them, and I'm going to fill my apron with corn, and they'll all come running to me!'

'I should not become too involved with them, Rosie dear,' advised Mrs Bagthorpe, worried by this speech. 'They are not to be pets, remember, but productive members of the ménage. They are coming for a *purpose*.'

Rosie had clearly overlooked the undoubted fact that these hens, having produced their eggs, would almost certainly end up in a casserole. (Given that they were able to bypass Daisy.)

'I've thought of lots of names already,' she continued happily, appearing not to have heard what her mother had said. 'Biddy and Cluck and Speckles and Blackie. But I'll wait till I see their faces before I decide, so's they'll have names to really suit them.'

Mr Bagthorpe rose.

'Cease your prattling,' he told Rosie. 'Those hens are here to lay eggs, not to feature in a Walt Disney film. And you, William, get on to that prophet fellow in Grimsby and see if you can't get him to catch some kippers. We're clean out of them. Tell him to let his everlasting Alien Intelligence get on with it by itself, and get catching some kippers.'

'You don't catch kippers,' William told him.

Mr Bagthorpe stared at him.

'Shoot them perhaps?' he inquired sarcastically.

'There are no kippers in the sea,' William said.

'Look,' said Mr Bagthorpe, 'I may not be the Brain of Britain, but I do happen to know that the North Sea is full of kippers, and that Grimsby is the place where they pull 'em all in.'

William, who was in no mood to explain to his father the processes whereby a herring becomes a kipper, himself rose.

'I am glad you reminded me of the Brain of Britain,' he said. 'It's on tonight. I'm going to have one last shot at blacking the wavelength.'

'Do you really think you should, dear?' Mrs Bagthorpe was anxious about this. She genuinely believed that her elder son was capable of plunging Britain into total silence on the Radio Two network, and was fearful of the repercussions of this action.

'Just leave it to me, Mother,' William told her loftily. 'No need to get in a stew.'

He went out.

'Stew!' came Mrs Fosdyke's disillusioned voice. 'That'll be the day . . .'

Chapter Eleven

The day the hens arrived was an active one even by Bagthorpian standards. It was lucky that Mrs Fosdyke was not there to witness most of the happenings. She was dismissed after lunch by Mr Bagthorpe.

'Take the afternoon off,' he told her. 'I shall need the kitchen.'

'Why is that, dear?' inquired his wife nervously.

'I am going to brew beer,' he announced.

'But, Henry,' she protested, 'you do not know how to brew beer.'

'It's easy,' he told her. 'Any fool could do it. I'm going to make eight gallons. And I may as well tell you I'm going to make rhubarb wine as well.'

'I do not consider wine and beer to be essential to Survival,' Tess told him. There was currently precious little sweetness and light in her own life, and she did not see why there should be in his. 'They are luxury commodities.'

'Bilge,' said Mr Bagthorpe. 'They are life-enhancing, and, as such, part of Survival.'

The rest of the family thought the logic of this shaky, but did not trouble to say so. If Mr Bagthorpe said he was going to brew beer and wine, then he would do it.

'It is to be hoped, Henry, that you do not blow up the house in the process,' Grandma now remarked.

Grandma counted as lost all time not spent either conducting a row or planning how to stage one. She was on this occasion rewarded by the expression on Mrs Fosdyke's face, which was one of undiluted horror.

'Blow up?' she echoed. 'My kitchen?'

'I shall blow nothing up,' Mr Bagthorpe stated with a confidence shared by no one else there present.

'I have certainly read in the press of cases of severe injuries inflicted in the process of amateur wine-making,' Grandma continued. 'And you, Henry, are nothing if not an amateur. You are scarcely able to brew a pot of tea without incident.'

'If my kitchen blows up,' Mrs Fosdyke said, 'there'll be no point my coming here any longer, if you'll excuse me saying, Mrs Bagthorpe.'

'Oh really, Mrs Fosdyke,' Mrs Bagthorpe protested. 'There is absolutely no question of such a thing happening.'

Mrs Fosdyke was little comforted by this assurance, knowing, as she did, that her employer was an incurable optimist – as, indeed, she needed to be as head of so accident-prone a ménage.

'That's what you said about the dining-room,' Mrs Fosdyke reminded her. 'You said history never repeated itself, and it did. History's always repeating itself round here.'

'I think it would be prudent if we were all to vacate the house while the brewing is in process,' Grandma said. 'Though if my memory serves me correctly, the explosions do not tend to take place during the actual brewing, but at a later date, and quite without warning.'

'That's marvellous, that is!' William said. 'We're already bags of nerves and skin and bone from all the muck we've been eating, and now we're told we're sitting on an active volcano. That is just about all we needed.'

'You are being silly, William,' his mother told him. 'Think, Rosie, your hens will be here at any moment!'

This transparent attempt to steer conversation away from the subject of explosions within earshot of Mrs Fosdyke met with total failure. Daisy had so far taken no part in the conversation, but now, having assessed the situation, made her own contribution to the general jumpiness of the company.

'If the house blowed up,' she remarked pensively, 'everybody could be dead. And if everybody was dead, just *fink* how many funerals I could have!'

Nobody but Daisy herself wished to think about any such contingency, even Grandma. The latter, however, thought this was a promising line along which conversation could be steered.

'Certainly you could, Daisy,' she said. 'Though you and I must ourselves beware that we are not victims. Perhaps we should take our meals in my room.'

Grandma's Fortnum and Mason hamper was up there, anyway, as a precaution against pilfering by her ravening and unscrupulous relatives, and Daisy herself was still quite chubby, having come in for a good share of the delicacies.

'I'm off!' Mrs Fosdyke was by now thoroughly disgusted. 'And it's to be hoped when I come in tomorrow I'll find my kitchen as I left it!'

This sounded like a threat. She slammed out.

'Those that can't stand the heat should get out of the kitchen!' Mr Bagthorpe said delightedly. 'And that applies to the lot of you!'

They scattered willingly enough. William was supposed to be putting the last touches to the hen-run, and dealing with its occupants on their arrival. Instead, he sneaked back up to his room for a final desperate bid to jam one of the BBC's radio networks. He accordingly was later held responsible for much of the pandemonium that ensued, though in fact very many people were to blame, including Mr Bagthorpe himself.

Mr Bagthorpe started brewing his beer, and then remembered that he had heard somewhere that if extra sugar is added, the resulting mixture will be much more potent. He understandably felt that he would be in frequent future need of such a brew, but found no sugar in the pantry.

'You go and get some,' he told Rosie, who was hanging around the outside, for the arrival of her chickens. She protested strongly at this, but there was no one else within call (or if there were, they were lying low) and she was despatched none the less.

No sooner had she gone than the chickens arrived. Mr Bagthorpe was reading a book about edible berries, and did not wish to be interrupted.

'Just bang 'em down there,' he told the man. 'We'll sort 'em out later.'

'You'll 'ave to pay a deposit on the cages,' the man told him. 'Returnable when you send 'em back.'

With ill grace Mr Bagthorpe forked out the deposit and returned to his book. Not many people who brew beer sit reading books at the same time. They stir continuously, as advised in the recipe. Mr Bagthorpe, however, in common with his offspring, had a very low boredom threshold. He was not the kind of man to stand round stirring over a low heat. He had never, in fact, followed a recipe in his life, and hated to be given instructions of any kind. He tended to rely on inspiration. Accordingly, he turned the hot plate up full, and left the beer to its own devices.

He was so engrossed in his book that he did not notice Daisy's passage through the kitchen, nor hear her reception of the hens. She was enchanted by these, but very upset to see them in cages.

'Poor little hens!' she said to them. 'It's not fair to be in cages. You should stretch your wings and fly away like the eleven swans.'

For Daisy, to think was to act. The catches of the cages were simple to unfasten, even for her small fingers. The hens wandered out on to the drive, and started pecking at the gravel. This in itself would not have mattered if two further developments had not followed closely. The first was that Jack appeared on the scene, followed by Zero, and the second was that Mr Bagthorpe's beer boiled over.

Zero had never seen hens before. He never did much chasing of cats or rabbits. The only things he had ever been interested in chasing had been squirrels. Jack later said that he thought hens were squirrel-shaped, and Zero had become confused by the likeness, but no one else could see this.

'If that infernal hound cannot distinguish a hen from a squirrel,' Mr Bagthorpe fulminated, 'then you should get some shears and lop some of that matted fur from over its eyes. *I* couldn't see under fur like that. Nobody could.'

For whatever reasons, then, Zero became very excited and started to chase the hens. The effects of this were very gratifying, and Zero rapidly became delirious, hardly knowing which way to turn next. The hens scampered frantically hither and thither and one or two of them managed to get back in their cages. Three of them, running in convoy, ran straight through the open kitchen door, pursued by Zero. This was at the precise moment that Mr Bagthorpe's beer boiled over.

All hell then broke loose. Zero, barking wildly, was still chasing the hysterical hens. He bounded straight into Mr Bagthorpe, who skidded in some spilt beer and went headlong. He lay there yelling and cursing, and Jack vainly tried to catch Zero, and the beer went on boiling. Two of the hens then flew up, one on to the table, where it knocked over a half-full bottle of wine and a jug of marigolds. The other hopped from a chair to the dresser, where it ran up and down flapping and squarking and soon dislodged, inevitably, the replica of the replica of Thomas. The crash was spectacular. It was, Mr Bagthorpe later said, the only good thing to have come out of the whole débâcle. Grandma, having given much thought to the positioning of this dubious ornament, had finally opted not for the place of honour in her own room, but for the dresser.

'Where we can all enjoy it,' she said.

Most people were surprised by this, but not so Mr Bagthorpe.

'Mother knows full well,' he declared, 'that the sight of that repellent ginger pot will put us all off our food. She has deliberately, and with diabolical intent, chosen the place where it will cause most suffering.'

He had even threatened to knock it off himself once or twice, and was certainly inclined to congratulate the hen responsible for its destruction.

This, however, was the only congratulation to be made by anybody to anybody, and for hours after the incident recriminations were flying on a scale never before known. Insults were exchanged, characters denigrated and voices had to be raised to an almost supersonic level in order to be heard at all. Every single person in the household was in a passion for one reason or another.

Grandma was fuming about the fall of her pot Thomas, and accused Mr Bagthorpe of deliberately engineering the whole thing, quite overlooking the undoubted fact that it had been Daisy, and not he, who had set the hens free. Even after this had been pointed out she persisted in her accusation.

'If you had done the humane thing,' she shrieked, 'and taken those hens straight to their run, none of this would ever have happened. Of *course* Daisy freed the birds from those barbaric cages. She cannot endure the sight of suffering, and is a lover of all creatures great and small. I am proud of her, and I am utterly ashamed of you, my own son, who stood callously by, brewing intoxicating liquor, while a little innocent child strove to redress wrong!'

She made Mr Bagthorpe sound like the villain of a Victorian melodrama. She was, of course, secure in the knowledge that she had the backing of most of the family, though they were less elaborate in their phrasing.

'If you hadn't sent me for that stupid sugar I'd've been there!' Rosie screamed. 'They're *my* chickens, and now you've frightened them, and they might not lay any eggs now for ever and ever!'

'Amen,' added Daisy automatically, but no one heard this.

The issue of the chicken's future egg output was not at the time considered vital by anyone but Rosie herself.

'To *hell* with eggs!' Mr Bagthorpe yelled. 'What about my beer?'

Mr Bagthorpe's beer, or what remained of it, was going, patently, to be undrinkable. If it tasted anything like what it smelled, it was probably poisonous. The smell of burnt sugar and yeast is not a pleasant one, and William actually volunteered the opinion that it was sniffing this that had sent Zero and the hens out of their minds.

'It's enough to make anyone blow their mind,' he said, pinching his nostrils. 'Pooh!'

There was blackened beer all over the stove, and when the obnoxious brew was seized and poured down the sink by Mrs Bagthorpe there was discovered to be a solid crust of burned yeast and sugar on the bottom of the pan. This was the inevitable result of Mr Bagthorpe's lack of conscientiousness in the matter of stirring.

'How shall we remove it?' she wailed. 'Oh – it is Mrs Fosdyke's best jam pan. Whatever will she say?'

Mr Bagthorpe consigned Mrs Fosdyke to Hades with the same fine disregard he had shown the eggs, and announced his intention of brewing again, immediately.

'If I do not, I shall lose my nerve,' he asserted.

During the stunned lull produced by this announcement Tess, who had not been missed in the general pandemonium, entered, herself in a stare of near-hysteria. So distraught was she, that she actually used words of few syllables, like ordinary people. She was graphic to an unprecedented degree.

'Get your beastly hens off my patch!' she screamed at Rosie. 'You get them off this minute! All my plants! All my plants – they'll be dead of shock, every one of them. Go on! Go on, I tell you!'

Here she stamped her foot. The Bagthorpes were impressed by this uncharacteristic performance, though no one had the least idea what she was talking about.

'You haven't *got* any plants!' Rosie screeched back. 'You leave my hens alone! You only *sowed* them yesterday!'

Jack himself thought that Tess was over-reacting, and it was some time before the reason for her outburst became clear. She had lately, they were vaguely aware, been much caught up in the paranormal. She had been reading, for instance, a good deal of Lyall Watson. From this she had become drawn to several theories, all of them described by Mr Bagthorpe, who was a fine one to talk, as half-baked. One of these theories was about the sensitivity of plants, and how they reacted to what went on around them. From all accounts, seeds were a good deal more sensitive than the Bagthorpes themselves.

Her day-old seeds, Tess maintained, as well as those germinating after being sown a week previously, had been subjected to the 'threat to well being' principle. She insisted on describing in detail certain experiments in which plants had been tortured, by having their leaves dipped into a cup of hot coffee, for instance. These plants had all been wired up to a lie detector, to measure their emotional reactions, and at the mere touch of the scalding liquid, she said, their tracings had risen dramatically. Not only that, but apparently somebody had only to *think* about harming plants, and they would pick this up by telepathy, and react similarly. It was this that was called the 'threat to well being' syndrome. (Plants also cared deeply about shrimps, it emerged. When this experimenter had dropped live shrimps one by one into a pan of boiling water, this one particular rubber plant had fainted each time.)

Nobody believed a word of any of this, least of all Mr Bagthorpe, who had little time for other people's half-baked theories. He said that if there were really such a thing as the 'threat to well being' principle, then the Bagthorpe line would have become extinct long since.

'Everything that ever happens around here is a threat to well being,' he said.

'*You're* always talking about vibrations,' Tess told him, with perfect truth. 'And if you can pick up vibrations, so can plants!'

Mr Bagthorpe replied that if all this were true, then it was self-evident that the immediate environs of Unicorn

House would be totally devoid of plant life. They would be not so much a garden as a desert.

'Even a cactus could not survive on the vibrations emanating from this house,' he declared. 'And Fozzy's herb garden would sure as hell be flat on its back.'

Jack thought he had a point here, but not so Tess.

'Whether or not you wish to admit it,' she told her father, 'we are all part of the Cosmic Mind. Every violent thought you have is reverberating through the entire Universe.'

This was a considerable prospect. If it were true, Jack thought, it was a poor look-out for the Universe.

The long day wore on, with people finally abandoning their verbal onslaughts and scattering to repair the damage done and put themselves together again. It took Rosie and William a good three hours to capture all the roaming hens. At one time, it seemed that it might be a good three weeks, until they hit upon the expedient of using the now redundant strawberry net.

Daisy and Grandma retreated to the latter's room, and Jack took Zero to *his* room so that he would not become excited by the squirrel-shaped hens still loose in the garden. He then set off alone to the village, on Mr Bagthorpe's instructions, to purchase further supplies of sugar. Tess disappeared, presumably to talk soothingly to her shocked seeds.

Mr Bagthorpe relentlessly went on brewing beer. He used the second-best jam pan, while Mrs Bagthorpe energetically scraped and scoured the burnt one. She had just completed this labour by the time Mr Bagthorpe had all his ingredients tipped into his pan, and Jack returned with the sugar.

'There!' he exclaimed with satisfaction. 'That's broken the back of it. Keep stirring it, Laura, will you? I have just had this shattering idea, and wish to note it down before

128

it has gone for ever. Inspiration in this house dissolves like foam upon the deep.'

With these words he made his exit, leaving his spouse, her brow deeply furrowed, stirring hard with one hand and holding the book of brewing recipes in the other. After a time, tiring of this tedious exercise, she switched on the wireless, for light relief.

What she heard could in no way be described as light, nor did it give her any relief.

'It is the point at which it would be impossible for a body to get any colder, that is, at which it is totally devoid of heat. This is estimated at about $-273°$ Centigrade.'

Mrs Bagthorpe herself froze considerably at the sound of this piping, familiar voice.

'Absolutely right!' came the voice of the quizmaster. 'That is the exact definition of absolute zero, and you, Luke Bagthorpe, are winner, by one point, of the semi-final round of this Young Brain of Britain Contest, and will go forward to the final next month.'

Numbly, Mrs Bagthorpe turned off the radio. At Unicorn House, rock bottom, if not absolute zero, had now been reached.

Chapter Twelve

Much of the blame for Luke's success in his semi-final was cast upon Mr Bagthorpe himself. It was he who had given Zero his name.

'If there was anything less than zero, that hound would be it,' he had stated (wrongly, of course). 'But there isn't, so we'll settle for that.'

If Zero had not been given that particular name, the young Bagthorpes argued, then Luke would not have been moved to look up the definition of absolute zero, and would have lost this vital point. Also, had they not themselves been occupied repairing the ravages caused directly or indirectly by Mr Bagthorpe's ill-starred beer brewing, they would have been able to transmit wrong answers to Luke by sending out powerful thought waves, they said. Nobody but Tess herself actually believed this, it merely suited their purpose to say that they did.

Tess told them privately that they had better believe it, and that they had better practise the sending out of these thought waves if Luke was to be foiled. Some of them actually did, on the quiet, Jack himself included. He found the practice difficult, however, because it did not matter how powerfully he *thought* he was thinking, there seemed no way of measuring how far these thoughts were in fact travelling. He persevered mainly because he genuinely thought this would be a useful power to cultivate, and because he was impressed by the total conviction with which his elder sister was pursuing her theories.

One thing Tess was doing was talking to her plants. She was also playing music to them. She took, without permission, every portable radio and tape recorder in the house, and had these positioned at strategic intervals in her vegetable garden. Sometimes, of course, it rained, and William, whose equipment had been very expensive, and paid for out of his own pocket, did so much shouting in the vicinity of her vegetables that it must certainly have negated any therapeutic effects the music might have been having. Tess, doubtless realizing this, redoubled her efforts. She would turn all the available radios on to Radio Three, which offered a diet of classical music all day, interspersed with the occasional highbrow talk given in measured and cultivated tones. There was nothing on Radio Three that could upset any seedling, however young.

Tess developed extended theories of her own, such as, for instance, that courgettes responded better to Mozart and Haydn than to Beethoven. Lettuce, she maintained, had a partiality for Handel, while tomatoes stood up and fruited for Wagner. There was no way anybody could either prove or disprove these theories, but most people admitted to themselves, if not publicly, that Tess did seem to have green fingers.

'You have probably always had green fingers,' her

father told her, on one occasion when she was boasting of this herself. 'Your trouble is that your fingers have been for ever monkeying about twiddling oboe keys, instead of getting to grips with Nature, as they should have been.'

As it turned out, Tess's delight in her saladings and vegetables was to be short-lived. As the seedlings waxed and flourished on their regime of classical music and kind words, Tess began to compare their appearance with that shown on the seed packets from which they had been sown.

'*Lettuce*?' she was to be heard dubiously murmuring, and 'Surely this leaf formation is at odds with that depicted here?'

Nobody took much notice of this initially, but as her unease mounted, several of them were requested to come and themselves compare the pictures on the seed packets with the actualities sprouting among the canned music. Jack was asked to inspect the lettuce, and admitted that he did not recognize it as such. He had a fair idea of what lettuce should look like, with or without the aid of a seed packet.

'The funny thing is,' he told her, '*some* of them look like lettuce. Those bigger ones at the end do, and even one or two of these little ones. Perhaps they're a kind of variegated lettuce.'

'Don't be an idiot!' Tess told him. 'The ones at this end I sowed exactly a week later, as one is supposed to do, to ensure a regular supply. And they came out of exactly the same packet as the first ones. Do these look like radish to you?'

'Pull one up,' Jack advised. 'See if it's got pink at the bottom.'

Tess did so. The experiment was inconclusive.

'It's too early,' she said. 'They wouldn't be pink anyway, at this stage. It's the *tops* that are wrong.'

Mrs Bagthorpe was finally called in for an opinion. She tripped happily down the path to the mixed strains of the Mozart Horn Concerto No. 3 in E flat major, and the *Siegfried Idyll*.

'How perfectly splendidly you are doing, Tess,' she told her daughter. 'How straight you have kept your rows, and how marvellously healthy all your plants look. Do you know, I think you may even begin to add Gardening as a String to your Bow.'

Tess ignored her mother's effusion.

'These,' she said without ceremony, pointing to the putative lettuce. 'Are they lettuce?'

Mrs Bagthorpe looked slightly troubled. Although she pottered about a good deal in the flower garden, and was something of an authority on clematis and Old English roses, she had heretofore met salad only when it reached her kitchen. She peered closer, and her brow cleared. She was on home territory, it seemed, after all.

'Why, no, dear!' she cried. 'See – these are pansies, and these antirrhinums – and those, see, are certainly night-scented stock. The paler green ones I am not so sure about . . .'

'They're lettuce!' Tess snapped. 'And the others are *what*?'

Mrs Bagthorpe repeated her diagnosis with confidence.

'I have some night-scented stock at exactly the same stage myself,' she said (she was defying her husband's instructions to grow only what was edible). 'Daisy sowed them for me only last week. It may even be that *she* has green fingers, too.'

'Daisy? Daisy?' Tess's voice was on an ascending scale. 'If that pernicious, meddling, undisciplined –'

Jack tugged at her sleeve.

'Don't you think we ought to move away where the plants can't hear?' he asked. He had the feeling that harsh words were about to be spoken – as indeed, they were.

The kind of words used must have reverberated through the Cosmic Mind like anything.

Where the Bagthorpes had gone wrong was in assuming that Daisy could be in only one Phase at a time. It had simply not occurred to them that they might overlap. Thus Daisy, while currently in a predominantly Intimations of Mortality Phase, was none the less still dabbling in Reconciling the Seemingly Disparate – and, for all anyone knew, in pyromania. When Mr Bagthorpe learnt this he became frantic.

'My God!' he yelled. 'Get the matches rounded up, quick! All I need is for this place to go up in flames to *know* I'm in hell!'

The full extent of Daisy's crime emerged only gradually, though the effects of it were with them for a long time to come. To start with, apparently, all she had done was take a pinch of one kind of seed and drop it into a different packet. Given Daisy's tendency to extremes, however, this had soon begun to pall. It seemed altogether too tame. She had begun, it seemed, to feel like doing something more drastic.

'I wanted to be a witch and mix a spell!' she sobbed to the stony-faced Bagthorpes.

'Witch is right!' gritted Mr Bagthorpe. 'Didn't I tell you? Exorcism – two exorcisms!'

Daisy's next act, then, had been to trot back to the house and find a receptacle that bore some resemblance to a witch's cauldron. The nearest she could come to this was a valuable black Wedgwood bowl (later found in pieces behind the potting shed). Into this she had tipped the contents of every seed packet she could lay her hands on. These had included cabbage, sunflowers, asters, carrots, night-scented stock, lettuce, radish, marigolds, lobelia, alyssum, beetroot and nasturtium. Nobody ever discovered what the exact mix had been. The flowerbeds of Unicorn House presented a unique spectacle during the coming months, with lettuce nestling among the roses and herbaceous borders of a variety that could never before have been seen anywhere. Grandma said that it was original, and that she liked it, and that Daisy's policy should be adopted every year.

'We might even present it at the Chelsea Flower Show,' she said.

While the row about Daisy's spellmaking was going on it had occurred to Jack (who rarely took part in rows) that now, perhaps, with the vegetable garden sprouting inedible produce, Mr Bagthorpe might finally decide to abandon his Scheme for Survival.

Not so. People were now made to fill any spare moments on their knees in the vegetable garden, comparing seedlings with pictures on packets. This was work of astonishing tedium, and strained everybody's eyes.

Jack was glad when one morning Mr Bagthorpe dispatched him into Aysham with instructions to buy, beg, borrow or steal a book about how to milk goats, this information not being given in any of the library books William had fetched earlier.

'And don't come back without one,' he told Jack. 'We must get our goat.'

As it happened, Grandpa was driving into Aysham to purchase further supplies of angling gear. He had been sent fishing so often of late that his equipment was wearing out. The two of them drove in together, and held a companionable conversation. When Grandpa was away from Unicorn House he seemed able to hear much better than when in the thick of things.

'I was wondering if I ought to call in and see Great Aunt Lucy,' Jack told him. 'I bet she'd like a visitor.'

He had in fact been instructed to do this by his siblings.

'She is our last ditch,' William said. 'If this goes on much longer we shall all drop dead of malnutrition.'

'Yourself, presumably, rather later than the rest of us,'

135

Tess told him coldly, alluding to the exhumed chops.

'Please, Jack, be really nice to her,' Rosie pleaded. Her chickens were a disappointment to her. They did not behave at all like the birds of the forest in Walt Disney's version of *Snow White*. She had never really expected them to flutter about her head or perch cooing on her shoulders, but she had expected them to be more affectionate than they were. When she threw scraps they just ignored her and fought and pecked amongst themselves. Not one among them looked cosy and placid enough to be called Biddy. Rosie *had* given them names, but they never came when called, and so she found herself forgetting which was which. The only enjoyable part was picking out the eggs, still warm, from the nesting boxes. Even this she did not often get to do. Daisy liked doing it, and Rosie always let her because at least it wooed her away, temporarily, from Grandma and Little Tommy.

Mathematics was one of the Strings to Rosie's Bow, and she acquired a small notebook in which to keep a Record of eggs laid, with the intention of producing some kind of Statistics. Given Daisy's frequent visits to the hen house this was not easy. For one thing, Arry Awk dropped quite a lot of eggs, and did not own up unless he was caught out. For another, Daisy kept secretly burying eggs, in the hopes that they would hatch out. Nobody could convince her that this was impossible. She said that ostriches buried their eggs in the sand, and so hens ought to be able to bury theirs in the soil ('They might even hatch out into *dragons*!' she said with satisfaction.) Given all this, Rosie's Statistics were clearly to be taken with a pinch of salt.

Rosie had given Jack six brown eggs as an offering to Great Aunt Lucy, though needless to say her motives for this were less than altruistic.

'Make sure she knows I grew them myself,' she told him. 'It'll show I've got strength of character.'

Tess sent a tin of talcum powder from the vast store she had accumulated during her Competition Entering days. Jack also smuggled a bunch of flowers, which was to be an offering from William and himself, into Grandpa's car while Mr Bagthorpe was not looking. The latter, of course, had no idea of Jack's proposed visit.

Grandpa thought the idea of going to the hospital a good one.

'I will drive you there myself,' he told Jack, 'and will myself go and see how Lucy is. She is a very strange lady, and I am sorry for her.'

Jack fervently hoped that Grandpa would be wise enough not to tell Grandma about this. 'She'd kill him,' he thought, but comforted himself with the realization that Grandpa could not have survived as long as he had, if he had not had some idea of how to handle Grandma. His being SD was part of his way of coping, Uncle Parker said.

Grandpa certainly seemed to hear all that passed during the visit to Great Aunt Lucy's sick bed.

Jack had been worried that the ward sister might not let them in. However, he himself was not even recognised, Mr Bagthorpe and Daisy having stolen most of the limelight on the previous occasion, and Grandpa, of course, had not even been there. The sister greeted them quite warmly (probably because Grandpa had such a nice face) and even told them about Great Aunt Lucy's previous visitors.

'She will be so pleased to see you!' she said. 'Some quite *dreadful* relatives came to see her when she was first admitted.'

'She is happy, I hope?' Grandpa asked, 'and her health is improving?'

'Oh, she's *enormously* better,' the sister assured him with pride. 'I think, though perhaps it is not for me to say, that her stay here is working wonders for her in every way. And she is getting on famously with her fellow-patients.'

This sounded so unlikely that Jack wondered fleetingly whether they were all talking about the same lady. His fears were short-lived. Great Aunt Lucy, still under her hooped cage, greeted them both with a smile. This was a real shock. Jack had not seen her smile before.

'How very kind of you to come, Alfred,' she told Grandpa. 'And you, too, William dear.'

'Jack, actually,' he told her.

'Of course. Do forgive me. I fear that I have in the past been very remiss in the matter of taking an interest in others, and hope to make up for this in the future.'

Jack boggled. Great Aunt Lucy, he knew, did not believe in either the past or the future. The old lady could surely not still be under the influence of an anaesthetic administered over a week previously?

'There is still time,' she continued, 'to make redress.'

She had actually now used the word Time. It was all quite incomprehensible. Jack made an effort to bring her back to reality as she knew it.

'Here are some flowers from William and me.' He proffered the bouquet. 'And here is some lovely flavoured talcum powder from Tess, and some brown eggs from Rosie. She laid them herself,' he added, remembering his instructions.

'How generous you all are!' she exclaimed. 'And new-laid eggs! I shall have one, lightly poached, for my breakfast each morning.'

The plot, so far as Jack was concerned, was now dense. Aunt Lucy was having her breakfast in the mornings. He stared at her for some kind of visible clue. His gaze fell on the pin fastening her bed jacket. It was one of her brooch watches. It was showing the correct time.

'There is one thing, Lucy,' Grandpa was saying, 'you will not be troubled by wasps in here, I imagine. We are

138

coming to the time of the year when they seem everywhere. I do everything I can to keep them down, of course, but one cannot exterminate a whole species single-handed, unfortunately.'

'When I am better, I shall help you, Alfred,' she promised. 'I shall not be sufficiently agile to swat them, as I could in my youth, but I can sit with an aerosol spray on my lap, and exterminate any that come within range.'

Grandpa took up this offer gratefully.

'You will remember, of course,' he told her, 'that cousin Cecil in Sevenoaks died of a wasp sting, and these things do run in families.'

'I suppose they do,' she agreed.

'I am convinced that that is the way I shall go myself,' he confided. 'Unless it be under the wheels of Russell's car.'

'Oh, I do hope not!' she exclaimed. She was, however, in no kind of a lather. Only a couple of weeks back she would have been in a considerable lather at such talk, and probably added wasps to the Bees in her Bonnet. Jack, still studying her, had the feeling that she was peaceful as never before.

'I am so happy here,' she told them. 'Each day has a pattern. Everything goes like clockwork.'

She then proceeded to outline the routine of the hospital day. Each hour, each minute, was accounted for. At last, it seemed, the responsibility for Time had been taken out of Aunt Lucy's hands. She could lie back and leave it all up to other people.

'It is sheer heaven,' she said blissfully.

Mrs Bagthorpe, on a subsequent visit, learned from the ward sister the manner of Great Aunt Lucy's conversion. It was, it appeared, the sheer, relentless regularity of hospital routine, a routine that stops for no man, that had brought about the miracle. At first, Aunt Lucy had resisted strenuously. She had demanded meals at all hours, and kept on switching on her bed light each time it was turned off by the night nurse, and refused to have her pulse taken. Bees in Bonnets as vigorous as hers are not seen off without a struggle.

Hospital staff, however, have people where they want them. They have been trained to get patients organized. In the end, they always win. Great Aunt Lucy had been inexorably worn down. The first sign of this was when she meekly accepted kippers for breakfast, this being the first meal she had taken since her admission. From then on, she had succumbed with increasing happiness to every detail of the routine to which she was subjected. Now she was not even looking forward to her discharge.

'We will ensure that your life continues in a regular pattern,' Mrs Bagthorpe assured her. 'And once you have become accustomed to the rhythm, I am sure it will be with you for life.'

Mrs Bagthorpe really did have a gift for Positive Thinking. Anybody who could talk about life as lived at Unicorn House as either regular or rhythmic, had to be a Positive Thinker of titanic stature. They had to be the biggest Positive Thinker since Canute – or Icarus, even.

Chapter Thirteen

In view of the drastic turnabout in Aunt Lucy's world picture, Jack decided to confess to his father that he had been to the hospital. He had not, after all, been categorically forbidden to do so. He consulted his siblings first.

'Are you *sure*?' Rosie asked incredulously. 'She actually said *Time*?'

'Several times,' he assured her. 'She seemed to like saying it. And she even said she was glad she'd fallen over that sack of mushrooms. She said she would be grateful for all time.'

'Grateful?' interposed William quickly. This sounded promising. 'Well, make sure you tell Father that.'

Jack, then, passed on to Mr Bagthorpe the information about Great Aunt Lucy's conversion to Time, along with the manual on goat-keeping. Mr Bagthorpe was not comforted.

'Here!' he said, snatching the manual. 'Give me that! We have little time to tend Lucy's bees. We must get to immediate grips with the goat.' (This latter was an almost prophetic phrase, as it turned out.)

'But she really has changed, Father,' Jack persisted. 'She's gone all peaceful. And she's really grateful to us all, she says, and especially you for putting those mushrooms for her to trip over.'

'Look,' said Mr Bagthorpe, 'do not waste your time describing how Lucy feels to me. I have known her since before you were born. Here today, gone tomorrow – every benighted Bee in her Bonnet spins round in circles at the speed of light. Peaceful, you say. If you visit her again, she will probably attack you with a poker.'

Jack pointed out that hospitals do not have pokers, but Mr Bagthorpe dismissed this as a quibble.

'Poker – hatchet – what's the difference? You are missing entirely the point I am making. The point I am making is that the day Lucy thinks the same way two days running, will be the day pigs fly. Now get digging. And when I'm through with this book, *you* read it. When the goat gets here, it will want milking. Fast.'

Grandma was equally dismissive about Aunt Lucy's personality change.

'You do not surprise me in the least,' she remarked when she was told of it. 'Lucy has always struck me as quite unstable. I have always been profoundly grateful that she is no blood relation of mine.'

She looked pointedly at her son, who *was* a blood relation, and therefore, by inference, prey to the same instability.

'I fink Auntie Lucy's a silly old griffin anyway,' piped up Daisy.

'Of course she is, dear,' her grandmother assured her. 'That little child is more perceptive than any other single member of this household, including, I fear, yourself, Laura. Why do you not consult her about your Problems?'

'When that hell-raising infant is about,' Mr Bagthorpe said, before his wife had a chance to reply, 'Laura is so beset left and right by her own Problems that she rarely has time to attend to the others. That child is herself, so far as we are concerned, a Problem with a capital P the size of Purgatory. She is, to use the words of that half-baked theory of Tess's, a Threat to Survival. Burying chops, biting people's legs, mixing seeds, dropping eggs –'

'I di'n't!' Daisy squeaked indignantly, interrupting this catalogue. 'It's Arry Awk! I told you, di'n't I, Rosie? He's a bad boy, and *he* mixes seeds and drops eggs. He dropped *six* eggs, yesterday.'

'That,' said Mr Bagthorpe grimly, 'is tantamount to a confession. Keep the score, Rosie, and I'll get the cash off Russell.'

'Daddy don't care!' Daisy said, keeping her end up. 'Daddy's got lots and lots of money!'

This tactless statement must have hit home hard. Mr Bagthorpe, however, had only entered into the exchange with Daisy while temporarily off his guard, and now tightly compressed his lips and affected to read the cricket scores in his newspaper. (This *had* to be affectation. Mr Bagthorpe had only ever once attended a cricket match, and had hideously disgraced the whole family by triumphantly yelling 'Howzat?' every time a batsman, on whichever side, scored a run. In the end the umpire had come over and had a word with him. Mr Bagthorpe had maintained that he thought this expression a cricketing variant of 'Hurray!' or 'Huzzah!' This happened to be true, though you could see the umpire did not believe him. When, several balls later, a batsman was given out Leg Before Wicket, Mr Bagthorpe had stood up and yelled '*Now* who's shouting Howzat?' Soon after this Mrs Bagthorpe had claimed that she had a serious headache, and they left the ground.)

'There is more livestock arriving tomorrow, I understand,' remarked Grandma, who did not like to see a state of simmer die down.

'What's livestock, Grandma Bag?' asked Daisy, who had been told by her mother always to ask the meaning of words she did not understand.

'It is any creature that is alive, Daisy,' Grandma told her. 'Everything that lives and moves and creeps upon the earth.'

'Is maggots livestock?' Daisy asked.

'Naturally, dear,' Grandma replied, 'though I should prefer you not to dabble in these.' (She had herself been a victim of some of Daisy's previous maggots at the Family

Reunion Party, and her memories of this event were pain-
ful.)

'It's not *me* that wants maggots, Grandma Bag,' Daisy
said. 'It's Arry Awk. He ha'n't *got* no livestock, and he
wants maggots.'

Nobody much liked the sound of this, but they were
not seriously perturbed, inasmuch as they imagined that
Daisy would have no way of procuring such livestock
single-handed. Her previous ones had been raised in the
airing cupboard by William, during the Germ Warfare
on the Latter Day Saints.

'I should rest content with Little Tommy, dear,'
advised Grandma, who did not know this. 'He is fast becoming a shining jewel of a cat, and requires your constant companionship. Why, dear, do we not hold another
funeral, and bury Arry Awk?'

She had imagined this an inspired thought, and was not
prepared for the violence of Daisy's reactions to it.

'He in't dead, he's not, he's not!' she squealed. 'He's
my bestest friend in the whole world and he's *not* dead!
And *he* han't got a wrinkly face and short legs. He's not
never going to die, not till I do!'

Most present felt that the time for this double demise
could not come too soon. Grandma, however, alarmed
by the strength of the passions she had aroused, immediately tried to modify her position.

'Hush, dear,' she told her protégée. 'You have quite
misunderstood me. I was not for a moment suggesting
that Arry Awk was dead. I merely thought that he might
enjoy attending his own funeral.'

Daisy's sobs abated, and you could see that she was
attracted by this novel proposition.

'There are, after all,' Grandma continued cunningly,
'few people who can ever have done this. In fact, Arry
Awk is the only person I have ever known of who *could*
attend his funeral. It would be an historic occasion.'

At this Mr Bagthorpe made a strangled noise and left the room.

'It's all hopeless,' William said gloomily. 'He doesn't even believe that Aunt Lucy talks about Time all the time and is eternally grateful to us. Can't we get him to go and see for himself?'

'I think that would be most unwise,' his mother said hastily. 'We must give him Time. He must be allowed to work through his obsession with Survival.'

The Bagthorpes sat morbidly contemplating this prospect, and at that moment there came the sound of grinding gravel that meant Uncle Parker had arrived.

'It's Daddy, it's Daddy!' Daisy squealed. 'He can come to Arry Awk's funeral as well. *Everybody* can,' she added generously. 'And even Uncle Bag, even if he is a nasty Grook!'

Uncle Parker breezed in, accompanied by Aunt Celia.

'Hello, all,' he greeted them. 'Still Surviving, I see?'

'Only just,' William told him.

Aunt Celia passionately embraced Daisy who, as usual, struggled to get free.

'Listen, listen!' she cried. 'We going to have a big funeral today and it's going to be Arry Awk's! And Grandma Bag says it'll be *hysterical*!'

'By Jove!' Uncle Parker was clearly impressed. 'Arry Awk, then, has finally kicked the bucket. I feared we should never see the day. Congratulations, Daisy – or rather, of course, condolences. Think, Laura, Henry and I will be able to reduce our Insurance Premiums which were, one is bound to admit, becoming crippling.'

'No no no!' shrieked Daisy, infuriated that Arry Awk, just because he was going to have a funeral, should be presumed dead. 'He's *not* dead, he's not!'

'Really?' Uncle Parker was quite nonplussed. His daughter's Intimations of Mortality were apparently taking a devious turn. He was slightly shocked. 'We are going to bury him *alive*?'

Obviously he felt that even Arry Awk did not deserve this fate.

'No!' squealed Daisy. 'You're not *listening*! You tell him, Mummy! We're going to have a funeral for Arry Awk and he's going to *come* to it!'

Aunt Celia instantly renewed her attempts to embrace Daisy. Evidently she alone perfectly understood the situation

'It is wonderful!' she told everybody. 'The symbolism of the ceremony is almost too deep for words. We are to witness the Phoenix arising from the ashes!'

'Will it be a cremation, then?' Jack asked. He, for one, devoutly hoped that it would not. This could mean that Daisy would then be in *three* Phases at once, which was a mind-blowing prospect.

'So literal,' murmured Aunt Celia, meaning Jack. 'How rare and precious it is to see poetry in a little child. I am constantly being reminded of how I have, in Daisy, a being quite unique.'

There was nothing in this last statement with which anybody could quarrel, and nobody did.

'Even Little Tommy can come,' Daisy was now burbling. 'You come and see my little pussy now, Mummy and Daddy. He's getting bigger and bigger and got *ever* so long claws.'

Aunt Celia allowed herself to be led off to view what sounded like an ominously developing Little Tommy. Uncle Parker remained.

'I'll take a look at him later,' he promised Daisy. 'Little beggar!' he added, as the door closed behind the pair.

'I may as well tell you,' he continued, 'that the real object of our visit is to persuade Daisy to return home.'

There was at this intelligence a great sigh of relief from everybody except Grandma and Rosie.

'The truth of the matter is,' he told them, 'that her mother is pining for her. She could stop here for ever, so far as I am concerned, but you know how Celia is. She's also a touch concerned, to put it bluntly, that if Daisy stops much longer amongst you lot, she'll get all the poetry knocked out of her.'

'We are certainly all getting a lot knocked out of *us*,' William told him, as Mr Bagthorpe himself would have, had he been present.

'The point being,' Uncle Parker said, 'that Daisy has got herself pretty well dug in here, latterly. And is also considerably attached to her grandmother – as who can blame her?' He here gallantly saluted Grandma, who ignored him. 'An inducement is therefore called for. And so, what with one thing and another, and all of you on a diet of beetroot and whatever, we thought of holding a Banquet.'

The Bagthorpes were rendered quite blank by this.

'We are calling it a Banquet,' Uncle Parker told them, seeing their surprise, 'partly because it will indeed be a Banquet, with every gastronomic delicacy in or out of season, and partly because Celia has now become irremediably nervous at the very sound of the word party.'

Given the long Bagthorpe history of making a clean sweep of party tables and usually burning out their locality to boot, this was hardly surprising. The Bagthorpes, however, were still not clear what exactly was being mooted.

'Do you mean a homecoming party for Daisy?' Rosie asked.

'That,' he replied, 'is precisely it.'

'At your house?' she asked incredulously. 'At *The Knoll*?'

'Where else?' he returned.

'But what about Aunt Celia?' Jack asked. 'What about her vibrations and things?'

Aunt Celia shared with Mr Bagthorpe an immovable conviction that people gave off vibrations. Given the kind of unsettled childhood they had probably had with Grandma, this was not perhaps surprising. Mr Bagthorpe's main obsession was with his study. He was very funny about whom he would let in, and had once even stopped the vicar entering. He was so frightened of the effect Mrs Fosdyke would have on the vibrations in there, that he actually hoovered and dusted it himself. He said this was because there were important papers that must not be disturbed, but his family knew what the real reason was. It was probable that Mrs Fosdyke did as well. Mr Bagthorpe by and large discouraged all visitors from Unicorn House by dint of shouting and general want of hospitable behaviour.

He did not, however, place an embargo on visits from the Parkers. Aunt Celia's vibrations, he claimed, were so wishy-washy as to be virtually non-existent, and Uncle Parker's so superficial as to be likewise. The main reason he let them come, however (he did not, after all, under-estimate the power of *Daisy's* vibrations) was that he and Uncle Parker carried on this long-standing feud. They would conduct frequent and protracted rows, and Mr Bagthorpe usually made notes afterwards, and used some of the dialogue in his television scripts. Uncle Parker had once threatened to sue him over this, on the grounds that anything he, Uncle Parker, might say was copyright.

Aunt Celia's obsession with vibrations was of a different order from that of her brother. She was affected by *everybody's* vibrations, though she did, as Mr Bagthorpe once sardonically pointed out, seem to have a remarkable immunity to those of her unholy daughter. Aunt Celia had then replied that he was confusing vibrations with charisma, which shone out from Daisy, she claimed, like a halo.

Aunt Celia spent a lot of time writing poetry and

throwing pots, or else thinking about these activities. She would spend hours just gazing at things. Uncle Parker let her because he loved her to distraction. He protected her as far as possible from the rest of the world's vibrations, but she was so easily upset that she would often have to lie for hours in a darkened room after hearing a harsh word spoken.

The Bagthorpes, then, had not for years crossed the threshold of The Knoll, apart from the odd occasion when Mr Bagthorpe had gone storming up there uninvited, having just thought of a scoring shot in whatever was the current battle of words. Uncle Parker had told them that they could not be invited there because of the threat it would present to his wife's sanity.

'Your combined vibrations,' he had said, 'are, you will concede, formidable. I do not necessarily say malignant – but formidable.'

Nobody cared much whether they visited The Knoll or not, and so the absence of invitations to do so had never given the Bagthorpes much pause, and the present summons was naturally something of a shock.

'This really is most kind of you, Russell,' Mrs Bagthorpe now said. 'How exciting it sounds – a Banquet!'

Here Mrs Fosdyke was heard to snort. She was probably trying to convey her conviction that the disasters attending a Bagthorpe Party were in direct proportion to its ambitiousness. At this rate, a Banquet could easily involve fatalities – of which there had been none so far. (Banquets were quite frequently featured in her Friday night Dracula films, and had therefore already become associated in her mind with dismemberment and much blood.)

'How many courses does a Banquet have?' inquired William with interest. 'Don't we keep eating courses till we're cramful, and then make ourselves sick to make room for more?'

149

'Something like that,' Uncle Parker agreed. 'Though I hope you'll all have the grace to be sick out of the sight of Celia.'

'Will there be a boar's head?' Rosie wanted to know.

At this, Mrs Fosdyke again snorted. She considered herself the best producer of party fare in the country, if not the world, but had never to date even considered a boar's head. She had only a confused notion of what it was.

'Anyone'd think,' she told Mesdames Pye and Bates in the Fiddler's Arms that night, 'that that lot'd never ate in their lives. The food I've given 'em! I've done 'em enough stuffed eggs in my time to build the Eiffel Tower with, and the gateaux I've done'd stretch to Land's End. Boar's head! I reckon I've *seen* some of them, at least, I think I 'ave, on them 'orrible banquets on Dracula, and I reckon they're 'orrible great enormous things with snouts and jelly all over and oranges in their mouths instead of teeth.'

Her cronies shuddered sympathetically at this description.

'Whatever next!' exclaimed Mrs Pye. This was a purely rhetorical remark, but Mrs Fosdyke went inexorably on to *tell* them whatever next.

'They was all *ordering* that Mr Parker what they wanted, as if they was a bunch of cannibals. All fancy foreign stuff it sounded and talking about syllabubs and venison and spits – oh, you can't imagine!'

'And will that wife of his do all that?' inquired Mrs Bates incredulously. She had often heard Mrs Fosdyke's assessment of Aunt Celia, which was, by and large, that she was 'only half there'.

'*Her*?' echoed Mrs Fosdyke. 'She could no more stick an orange in a pig's mouth than she could fly! One of them vegitarians – I *told* you – never hardly touches anything but lettuce.'

She went on to tell them what she had heard Uncle

150

Parker explaining to the Bagthorpes, which was that, as Aunt Celia was so highly strung and easily unhinged at the sight and smell of strong meat, a firm of London caterers was being called in to make all the necessary culinary arrangements. He had then, realizing that Mrs Fosdyke was within earshot, and that her sensibilities might be bruised by hearing all this, gone on to invite herself to attend, in a supervisory capacity.

'Keep an eye on things, you know,' he told her. He had a fair grasp of psychology (he needed to have) and knew how to butter Mrs Fosdyke up. 'And to tell you the truth, the one thing I really hanker for is a supply of your remarkable stuffed eggs. Could teach that lot a thing or two!'

'Shall you go, then?' asked Mrs Fosdyke's friends eagerly.

'Oooh, I should, Glad,' urged Mrs Pye. 'They say it's like Buckingham Palace inside.'

Who 'they' were was not clear, given Uncle Parker's reluctance to let people and their vibrations over the threshold of The Knoll. To Mrs Fosdyke, the Parker residence sounded very little like Buckingham Palace. She well knew that Daisy Parker was allowed to write her thoughts on the walls, and had started several fires there during her Pyromaniac Phase. It seemed unlikely that the royal children had ever been granted these prerogatives. But Mesdames Pye and Bates were dedicated inspectors of the interiors of other people's houses, even if they sometimes had to settle for second-hand accounts rather than a personal inventory. They might have acquired some information from somewhere.

Mrs Fosdyke allowed her friends to urge her acceptance for a little longer, and then assented with a show of reluctance.

'S'pose I might as well,' she told them. 'If all that foreign stuff ain't fit to eat they can always fall back on my

151

stuffed eggs.' (Mrs Fosdyke really did have an unconscious gift for prophecy. She had not meant this last statement literally at all.)

Next day, then, Mrs Fosdyke indicated her willingness to attend the Homecoming Banquet at The Knoll, with the proviso that there should be no candles and no crackers.

'A Banquet by its very nature does not have crackers,' Mrs Bagthorpe assured her. 'And as the evenings are still light, there will be no need of candles. I am sure the occasion will pass off beautifully. We are all so looking forward to it.'

They were – even Mr Bagthorpe, though he would not admit to it.

'It is like Russell,' he declared, 'to take a sledgehammer to crack a nut. Surely to God he could have rehabilitated his daughter without this kind of a masquerade. I may or I may not go. It will depend whether I feel I can face such rich and unwholesome food after a taste of nutrition as it should be.'

He had been given an outline of the proposed courses of the Banquet, and was very dismissive about them.

'We shall all be furred up for weeks afterwards,' he said. 'Menus of that order are totally out of date. They were drawn up when people knew nothing of cholesterol and polysaturated fat and vitamins.'

Mr Bagthorpe, of course, *still* knew very little about these matters, but he was not the man to let this stop his delivering a lecture about them. Mr Bagthorpe could deliver a lecture about anything, given one or two half truths.

Chapter Fourteen

The funeral of Arry Awk took place that afternoon with due pomp and ceremony. It had been postponed from the previous day with the arrangement of this pomp and ceremony in mind. Most people attended in the end, optimistically imagining that this was a finale, the *pièce de résistance* to mark the end of Daisy's Phase of Intimations of Mortality. Even Uncle Parker went. You never knew, he said, Arry Awk might accidentally fall into his own grave, and that he would not want to miss.

In the event, he was not far short of the truth. To begin with, things went smoothly enough. Daisy trotted round her procession inspecting its members and making sure everyone was wearing some black and carrying a floral tribute. She herself was bearing a bunch of flowers and foliage almost as big as herself, tied with pink ribbon and having a card attached that read 'Goodby Arry Awk my bestest frend in the hole world for evver and evver amen'. She had also appropriated her most original monument to date, in the shape of a giant glass jar of green bubble bath which would serve, she said, to remind Arry Awk of his lovely flood. His epitaph she had already composed in private, and intended to attach it with ribbon to the neck of the jar at the end of the ceremony.

She had insisted that Arry Awk be buried away from what was by now known as the Highgate Cemetery end of the garden. She was probably dimly aware that, even in death, Arry Awk was something on his own.

'It is as though,' crooned Aunt Celia dotingly, 'the darling child has unconsciously recognized the need for a Poet's Corner.'

Mr Bagthorpe elected, predictably, to give the funeral a miss, even though Daisy had magnanimously said he could attend. William, too, was absent, there being no possibility of later disinterring Arry Awk and having *him* with mint sauce. He was not even prepared to toll the bell, so Rosie volunteered for this duty. Unfortunately, she had not acquired the knack of tolling a handbell, and the resulting sound was more like a summons to school dinner than a solemn call to mourning. The vibrations of this clanging got on everybody's nerves in the end, with the astonishing exception of Aunt Celia, who, one would have imagined, would have been the first to clap her hands over her ears.

'No man is an island entire unto himself,' she was heard to murmur. And 'Never send to know for whom the bell tolls, it tolls for thee.'

She was presumably somewhere so far off on her own that she was not even hearing the vibrations, let alone feeling them.

The spot Daisy had selected for the laying to rest of the imaginary remains of Arry Awk was at the edge of the shrubbery, near a flowering rhododendron. (This imaginary side of things was very confusing to everybody except Daisy herself, and her mother. So far as the Bagthorpes were concerned, Arry Awk had always been imaginary and invisible, and it was weird the way Daisy seemed to think he was imaginarily in the empty toffee tin, but actually in pride of place in the procession at her side.)

'Come on, Arry Awk,' she said, instituting the proceedings, 'you jus' walk along with me. Walk in slow steps, and don't talk – jus' sing.'

The cortège set off, wailing in a dirge-like way. Daisy had said they could all sing anything they liked, so long as it was sad. Simultaneously and mercifully the bell stopped tolling, as Rosie dropped it in favour of her high-speed camera. She kept darting about ahead of the procession and filming. She had obtained permission for this seemingly disrespectful behaviour from Daisy.

'All historical funerals have photos taken of them,' she had told her. 'It'll make this funeral immortal.'

The others had heard this, and became even more confused by immortality being added to an already inextricable mixture of what was invisible, imaginary and real. The result of this was that hardly anybody among the mourners had any clear conception of what they were supposed to be burying.

They wound their way slowly to Poet's Corner and then halted, still singing, while Daisy got down to business with her trowel. Jack found himself, all at once, understanding what Rosie saw in her. She was so serious – almost dedicated – in whatever she was doing. He cast his eye over the other mourners, almost daring them to giggle. No one as yet showed any signs of doing so, nor were they to do so later.

'There!' Daisy stood up and surveyed her hole with satisfaction. 'You can stop singing now.'

This they obediently and thankfully did.

'This is the funeral of Arry Awk that Arry Awk has come to,' Daisy announced. 'It is a hysterical funeral. There will never be another, not for ever and ever amen.'

She looked about her fellow-mourners for corroboration of this, and they all nodded and assumed appropriate expressions of awe and solemnity.

'There is no need for anybody to cry,' Daisy then told them, 'because Arry Awk i'n't dead. He's here, i'n't you, Arry Awk?' She paused. Then, 'Yes, he is,' she confirmed. 'I will now put him in his coffin. He choosed it himself.'

She picked up the polythene bag and the toffee tin and went through the motions of placing something inside. Her audience all craned forward to see what it was, and for a fleeting moment Jack almost expected to catch a glimpse of Arry Awk himself. He was disappointed. What was actually standing proxy for this invisible person was some kind of blue plastic troll out of a cornflake packet.

Daisy held the tin aloft in her usual manner.

'Oh dear oh dear!' she cried. 'Poor Arry Awk! No more floods and no more eggs! Gone to heaven for ever and ever amen!'

This was all very baffling – and not only in Daisy's confident assignment of her friend to heaven. The Bagthorpes had only a moment ago been instructed that any outward show of grief would be misplaced, yet here was Daisy herself giving every sign of getting into her usual stride, and acting very bereaved indeed. She seemed to have forgotten that Arry Awk was there at her side, witnessing the whole thing. As Jack watched, her face crumpled and tears began to roll down her cheeks.

'Poor little fing!' she was sobbing in earnest now, as she placed the toffee tin into her newly dug hole. 'Oh, dusters to dusters, ashes to ashes! Oh dear, oh dear – Mummy, Mummy, I want him back!'

Aunt Celia, herself weeping, cried:

'No, darling, no! He is not dead, but sleeps!'

'He's dead, he's dead!' wailed Daisy.

Her grief was so real that everyone present began to feel affected – even Grandma, who had always been jealous of Arry Awk's place in Daisy's affections, and would have been only too happy to see him dead.

Daisy was now scattering forlorn little fistfuls of earth on to her tin.

'Oh Arry, Arry,' she sobbed, her face besmirched with soil and tears. 'Don't leave me, Arry! Oh dear – dusters to dusters!'

Uncle Parker, impressed by the way things were going,

ventured to put his oar in. He patted his daughter gently on the back.

'Look, Daisy,' he said, 'it's not too late. Fish him out again, why don't you?'

It must have cost him some effort to make this suggestion, because Arry Awk had always been a source of great trouble and expense to him.

'I can't, I can't!' screamed Daisy. 'He's dead! Oh, I wish I never done it! Darling little Arry Awk!'

Grandma, not wishing to appear deficient in feeling, but quite misjudging the depth of Daisy's despair, said:

'It's *always* a shame when somebody dies, Daisy. But you will soon have a new friend – and you have Little Tommy, remember.'

'I don't want Little Tommy,' Daisy screamed passionately, 'I want my Arry Awk back!'

'Don't cry, Daisy,' Jack said. 'Have you forgotten, Arry Awk is *with* you.'

'He i'n't, he i'n't,' she wailed. 'He's just gone down to ashes in that tin!'

The complicated metaphysics of the whole business had evidently become too much for her too, for she no longer seemed to understand it. She had on this occasion, as Mr Bagthorpe later unsympathetically observed, bitten off more than she could chew.

'Anybody who can go around burying people who are dead and alive at the same time has to *expect* to get tied up in knots,' he declared. 'Even Shakespeare never did that, and there's no reason why *she* should expect to get away with it. At least Shakespeare's ghosts were *dead*, for God's sake. Her whole diabolical creation has now ricocheted back on her. It is neither more nor less than poetic justice.'

It was in fact much later on that Mr Bagthorpe made this speech, because at the time when Arry Awk's funeral broke up in disarray, he was occupied in wrestling with a goat, and in no position to utter anything much more than expletives.

How the funeral finally broke up was with Daisy flinging down her floral tribute and fleeing, still sobbing bitterly. Aunt Celia instantly went after her, and the rest of them were left standing there awkwardly, uncertain of what their next move should be.

'Poor old Daisy,' said Jack at last.

'Perhaps it is all for the best,' said Mrs Bagthorpe weakly. (She had never received a Problem relating to Resurrection.)

'D'you think he *is* dead?' asked Rosie nervously. 'Had we better put our flowers on, or not?'

She had gone to some trouble to create a circular wreath, using wire clothes-hangers, beech twigs and roses.

'Better pop 'em on the hole,' Uncle Parker advised. 'Might cheer her up a bit when she sees 'em.'

This they all did, feeling much sadder than they had anticipated. Jack put the bath-salts jar at the head of the grave and propped Daisy's own floral tribute against it. As he did so, he spotted a crumpled piece of Grandma's lavender-scented notepaper. It was Daisy's special epitaph:

Only me knows Arry Awk
Only me can here him tawk.
I luv him and he luvs me
And hes as bad as bad can be.
Frinstance won day Arry Awk
Broke sum dums with a nife and fawk.
He had a flood and broke sum eggs
And he mixed up sedes wiv his twinkling legs.
Arry Awks my bestest frend
For evver and evver til the end
Amen.

Jack thought it clear from this composition that Daisy had not in fact contemplated losing Arry Awk in arranging his burial. There was no ring of finality about it – rather the opposite – and, significantly, no date. He himself thought Arry Awk sounded an attractive and lively character from this description, though he supposed that the twinkling legs attributed to him by Daisy were more or less poetic licence, there being few usable rhymes for 'eggs'. He carefully attached this eulogy to the neck of the bath-salts jar and followed the others, all of whom had already left the graveside.

Having been immersed in perusing the epitaph, he had not really noticed all the yelling and screaming up to this juncture, but now he automatically hurried in its direction.

'It really is all Hail and Farewell,' he thought.

So it turned out to be. Farewell Arry Awk was overlapping with Hail Jemima – this being the name already chosen in advance by Rosie for the Bagthorpe goat.

Mr Bagthorpe alone had been there to greet this addition to the livestock. William had his earphones on at the time, and so could not hear his yells and come to his assistance – even had he been inclined to do so.

Mr Bagthorpe had no kind of rapport at all with four-legged creatures. (He did not even have a marked rapport with *two*-legged ones.) His reception of the goat had been, then, initially lukewarm. He had been somewhat nervous of the animal, having heard about goats butting, and eating everything in sight. He did not, however, wish to lose face in the eyes of the delivery man, so he did not tether the goat at a distance and beat a hasty retreat, but held on to the end of its rope in what he thought to be a nonchalant and manly way.

'I'll soon settle it down,' he told the delivery man. 'I've got a way with animals.'

What he intended was to hold on to the rope just so

long as he was in view of the retreating van, and *then* tether the goat and beat a hasty retreat. Unfortunately, he left this too late. It was probably the noisy revving of the van, and the spinning of its wheels on the gravel, that upset the goat. Or it might, of course, have been Mr Bagthorpe's vibrations. In either case, the goat had become, so he averred, berserk. He went on to compare his own struggles with those of St George with the dragon.

'The only difference being that I shan't get a knighthood,' he added bitterly. 'There's no way I shall ever get a knighthood.'

When he was reminded that the George in question was a Saint and not a Sir, he became even more bitter, especially as he had been caught out.

'There is no way I shall ever get canonized, either,' he said, 'though I should be. I am a martyr, of the first water. I am the Archetypal Can-carrier of all time. St George can never have carried so many cans as I have.'

And so on and so forth. He was all the time tending his wounds, and allowing his wife to put the odd dab of antiseptic cream on his grazes, though he doubted, he said, whether these would afford any protection against possible rabies. Mrs Fosdyke wanted to put butter on all the bruises, but he would not let her. He said he considered this suggestion morbid.

'I need neither anointing nor embalming, as yet,' he told her coldly.

He was being particularly frigid toward her, partly because she had witnessed his humiliation by Jemima, and partly because she had not herself come to his aid. He had caught the occasional glimpse of her pop-eyed face during his protracted wrestling with the goat.

'She is yellow to the core,' he told his family after her departure. 'So much for loyalty. "Thy tooth be just as keen although it be not seen as benefits forgot," and all that. "Thy breath be not so rude as man's ingratitude."'

Jack thought this confused quote more than usually inept, in as much as Mr Bagthorpe had never, ever, so far as he knew, done anything to earn Mrs Fosdyke's gratitude. He even risked saying as much.

'And she might have been frightened, as well,' he added. 'And she's only little.'

Mr Bagthorpe then rounded on him.

'It is you,' he told him through clenched teeth, 'who will be milking that hellish thing. If you think you can do better, do. When you are black and blue from head to foot, you might remember those words, and have the grace to blush.'

Rosie giggled.

'Black and blue and red all over,' she said.

'Very funny. Jack, go and fetch that manual.'

Mr Bagthorpe clearly could not wait for someone other than himself to get to grips with the goat.

'See what time of day it wants milking,' he ordered, 'and how many gallons we're supposed to get. You'll keep milking till we get our full quota.'

In fact the Bagthorpes were to get no milk at all from the misnamed Jemima, who was a billy-goat. Anyone with the slightest knowledge of animals might have queried at the time of delivery a female goat without udders. This was not the kind of detail Mr Bagthorpe ever noticed, and it was his careless dismissal of detail that had resulted in the delivery of a goat of the wrong sex. He had been curt to a degree to the man on the other end of the line when ordering the animal.

Mr Bagthorpe was not in the habit of ordering goats. When the breeder started asking all kinds of questions about breed and other technicalities, Mr Bagthorpe had cut him off short, fearing that any further discussion would result in his revealing his own ignorance.

'Long-horned, short-haired – what's the difference?' he had said brusquely. 'Wednesday afternoon, please, without fail'– and slammed down the telephone.

Mr Bagthorpe really was his own worst enemy. If he had talked politely to the goat-breeder, he would at least have ended up with an animal of the right sex, of whatever breed. In the event, his rudeness was such that the man, who had the impression from something Mr Bagthorpe had said earlier in the conversation that it was a nanny-goat he was after, deliberately sent a billy. It was, after all, a very human reaction.

When the mistake was discovered, Mr Bagthorpe tried to bluster his way out of it.

'We'll eat it,' he said. 'We'll fatten it up on the spare grass and then eat it. Robinson Crusoe did it all the time. So did Ulysses. It will see us through the winter. We can use its blubber to make candles.'

The billy-goat did not meet this fate. Daisy came upon him while everyone else was in the house yelling or wailing. She had managed to elude her mother and was hiding in the shrubbery to grieve privately over her lost friend. There, through her tears, she saw, within inches of her own, the mild yellow eyes of the goat. (He had finally got his rope tangled round a shrub, and Mr Bagthorpe had managed to secure it with a hasty knot before lurching back to the house.)

Daisy's eyes blinked rapidly. *The Three Billy Goats Gruff* had always been one of her favourite stories. She used to make Uncle Parker keep reading it, in the hope that one day the troll *would* eat somebody. This was not because she had anything against billy-goats, simply that she liked to hear about blood-baths.

'Oooh!' she gasped. Her sobs abated. She stared at the goat and he stared unwinkingly back.

'You're a Billy Goat Gruff!' she exclaimed with awe. 'You got yellow eyes and a little tufty beard and horns jus' like in the book!'

The goat chewed thoughtfully.

'There i'n't no *troll*, is there?' she asked, looking fearfully about her. Daisy liked to witness bloodbaths, not participate in them.

'I sink p'raps we better go, case there is,' she told him. Her chubby fingers fumbled with the knot. In the end she managed to loosen it, and carefully unravelled the rest of the rope.

'C'm'on, Billy Goat Gruff,' she told him, and led him out of the shrubbery, over the lawns, and right into the mêlée in the Bagthorpe kitchen.

This was a stunning entrance. No one felt more stunned than Mr Bagthorpe himself. It was, moreover, hideously embarrassing. Here was the creature recently delineated by himself as voracious, cunning and even rabid, being led by a five-year-old like a lamb to the slaughter. The goat gazed mildly about him and took an exploratory chew at some rush matting. Mrs Fosdyke pressed herself right back against her sink. She had seen with her own eyes the other side of the goat's nature. She kept her eyes fixed on it, so that if it turned its gaze on herself, she could stare it out, as she had heard you were supposed to do with lions and pythons and so on.

'Oh Daisy, darling,' quavered Aunt Celia. 'Oh Russell – save her!'

'From what, dearest?' he asked. She was swaying slightly. He supported her, because if things became too much for her she would escape from them by fainting.

'Isn't he lovely?' Daisy inquired of the benumbed

Bagthorpes. She patted his head and he curled his tongue and looked pleased.

Grandma was the first to recover herself.

'Darling Daisy has tamed the ravening beast,' she observed. 'The wolf is lying down with the lamb.'

'Which,' gritted her son, rising to the bait, 'being which?'

Chapter Fifteen

Daisy was allowed to keep the goat, of course. Aunt Celia averred that it had been sent by Providence, in Daisy's darkest hour of need, tying it in with the Ancient Mariner in some incomprehensible way. She made what was, for her, a very long speech about it.

'He is the Phoenix who has risen from the ashes of Arry Awk,' she crooned. 'From henceforth, he will be Daisy's guide and mentor. He will protect her from all ills, as the lion protected the gentle Una.'

This hopelessly mixed-up assessment of what was, to all other eyes, a particularly destructive member of a breed noted for its destructiveness, irritated everybody, and most of all Mr Bagthorpe.

'Protect hell!' he shouted. 'That goat just damn near killed me, Celia. And the minute it gets itself together, it'll try killing again. Get it straight out of here. You owe me seventy pounds, Russell. You realize, don't you, that it'll probably kill your benighted daughter? You may, of course, think it cheap at the price.'

Daisy herself had no such misgivings, and was caressing her new pet non-stop.

'What a picture!' sighed Aunt Celia, in no way, now that her first shock was overcome, alarmed by her offspring's newfound affinity.

Grandma in turn became infuriated, not least because she was already experiencing powerful feelings of jealousy. She had expected Daisy to draw even closer to herself following the demise of Arry Awk, and now here she was, within the hour, showing every sign of becoming besotted with a goat.

'Picture!' she snorted. 'Are you deranged, Celia? The scene reminds me of nothing so much as Titania fondling Bottom with his ass's head. The child is bewitched. She has become possessed. Look at the creature's evil yellow eyes!'

'They *i'n't* evil!' Daisy now squeaked, having come to sufficiently to overhear this speech. 'Don't you *say* that, Grandma Bag! They're all lovely and yellow like bananas like in the book and I'm going to call him Billy Goat Gruff.'

'But, Daisy,' said Grandma, 'what about Little Tommy? Goats, I believe, particularly detest cats. What if the goat were to harm him?'

'I don't care!' Daisy answered. 'I like Billy Goat Gruff best. *You* can have Little Tommy. You keep him, Grandma Bag.'

The rest of the Bagthorpes paled at this offer.

'Certainly I think you should keep the cat, Mother,' Uncle Parker now smoothly interposed. 'He was, after all, intended as an offering to yourself from Daisy.'

'You keep out of this,' Mr Bagthorpe told him tersely.

Grandma, seeing her son's mounting fury, came to an instant decision.

'Very well, Daisy dear,' she replied, 'I shall keep the kitten. He has, after all, been responding well to his training, and is by no means the milk and water creature he was on his arrival. Thank you, dear.'

'Now *everybody's* happy,' said Daisy contentedly. 'I got Billy Goat Gruff and Grandma's got Little Tommy.'

This was a totally inaccurate assessment of people's feelings. Nobody was happy, unless, perhaps, the speaker herself. Quite apart from the prospect of having to live out their lives alongside a malevolent and unpredictable ginger tom, the younger Bagthorpes were now coming to realize that if Daisy were to depart happily with her newly acquired pet, then Uncle Parker's planned inducement to rehabilitate her at The Knoll would no longer be necessary. The Banquet, presumably, would be off.

William, who felt this as keenly as anyone, took the unprecedented step of offering advice on child-rearing to his aunt and uncle. He tried to sound dispassionate and wise in doing so.

'If I may be allowed to offer a word of warning,' he said, 'I really think it inadvisable to allow Daisy to have the goat. Daisy has a very symbolic mind, and the symbolism of a goat is not good. Not for a young child.'

This was a fairly cunning ploy, Jack thought, given the stress Aunt Celia always placed on poetry and symbolism. It nevertheless failed.

'The creature will have only that symbolism with which Daisy herself invests it,' replied Aunt Celia obscurely. 'She is her own mythmaker.'

'Oh my God!' Mr Bagthorpe exclaimed. 'Look, are you getting that animal out of here, or aren't you? Any minute now it'll start trying to kill again. And what about the seventy pounds?'

Here another argument set up. Uncle Parker declared that he had no intention of paying Mr Bagthorpe the full price of the goat.

'We are taking it off your hands, Henry,' he told him. 'You are scared out of your wits by it, and would probably pay money to rid yourself of it. I shall, however, take a fair view of the matter, and will give you half the sum you paid. I will, of course, wish to see the invoice.'

A real row now developed. Mr Bagthorpe was yelling and blustering even more than usual, because he on no account wanted Uncle Parker to see the invoice, which was for only fifty pounds, plus a delivery charge of three pounds. He had anticipated that Uncle Parker would try to knock a tenner off what he himself had paid, and with what he had smugly imagined was true financial wizardry had come swiftly up with a sum that would ensure that he would emerge from the deal in pocket.

Everybody present (except Daisy) was on Uncle Parker's side, in that in nobody's view was seventy pounds a realistic price for so unprepossessing an animal. The younger Bagthorpes kept shouting out their own estimates, ranging from fifty pence (William) to fifty pounds (Jack, who had believed his father's story about paying seventy).

The unexpected, however – the miraculous, even – was always tending to happen in Bagthorpian lives, and so now did the seemingly impossible occur. Daisy, sufficiently aware of what was going on to realize that the future of her Billy Goat Gruff was at stake, put her own oar in. She came heavily down on the side of Mr Bagthorpe. This made history.

'Daddy, Daddy!' she squealed, rushing toward him and tugging her goat after. 'Give Uncle Bag that seventy pounds! Give it him! You're mean! You got lots and lots of money and I want my goat, I *want* him! Mummy, Mummy, make Daddy give it Uncle Bag!'

There followed a stunned silence.

'There you are, Russell,' said Mr Bagthorpe at length, 'even Daisy acknowledges the animal's worth.'

It was a measure of his gratitude that this was the first time, so far as anyone could remember, that Mr Bagthorpe had been able to bring himself to allude to Daisy by name.

It was Daisy's appeal to her mother, of course, that settled the matter. Aunt Celia turned imploringly towards her husband, and laid a hand on his arm.

'Russell, dearest,' she murmured. 'For my sake . . .'

The next minute Uncle Parker was meekly fishing for his wallet and the transaction had been completed. It really was amazing, Jack thought, that Uncle Parker's

Achilles Heel should be Aunt Celia. One honestly would have thought he was made of sterner stuff.

Mrs Fosdyke made no secret of her own disgust when later describing the scene in The Fiddler's Arms.

'That Mr Parker's the only one of the whole bunch that's a proper gentleman,' she told Mesdames Pye and Bates, 'and what he was about, marrying that half-baked wife of his, I'll never know. There he is – like putty in her hands. Seventy pound! I ask you – seventy pound!'

The others clucked disapprovingly over their stout.

'And you never *saw* such a tussle as there was with that animal when it came! Saw it all, I did, from the window, and I swear to heaven I thought Mr Bagthorpe'd've got killed. Not that it wouldn't have served him right, but you don't expect goats to go round killing people. Nice headline *that*'d've made in the newspapers!' (Even Mrs Fosdyke, moving as she did only on the periphery of the Bagthorpes' lives, was becoming sensitive about headlines.)

'Anyhow,' she continued with satisfaction, 'it'll make an even better headline when the goat kills that Daisy. Which it will, sure as eggs. And at least their surname's Parker, and people won't go connecting it up with me, unless I tell 'em.'

'What about that banquit, Glad?' inquired Mrs Bates. 'Off now, is it?'

'On,' returned Mrs Fosdyke fatalistically. 'On. Said they'd done all the bookings now, and o' course all them children was clamouring terrible about the food. Then that Daisy said she wanted a party for that goat of hers, and that did it, o' course. That poor Mr Parker. However he came to be mixed up with that bunch of lunatics, is –'

'And what about that old woman in hospital?' asked Mrs Pye, interrupting this all too familiar line of speculation. 'Her that got us all tranquillized?'

'Don't *ask* me,' begged Mrs Fosdyke, none the less

going on to reply. 'They ain't *told* me anything, but I've got a 'orrible feeling she's getting better. And I've got a 'orrible feeeling she's even madder. There's some of 'em been to visit 'er – Mr Bagthorpe senior 'as, *and* Mrs Bagthorpe – junior, o' course – and from what *I* can make out, she's started believing in Time all over again! Now! What do you make of *that*?'

Her audience shook their heads, indicating that they could make nothing whatever of this heretical turnabout.

'Would you believe!' murmured Mrs Bates. 'Believes in *Time*!'

'It'll be for the worse,' said Mrs Fosdyke darkly. 'You mark my words.'

'Well, anyhow, Glad, you've got that Daisy out the 'ouse,' Mrs Bates told her friend encouragingly. 'You try and look on the bright side.'

It was not in Mrs Fosdyke's nature to look on the bright side, and even the departure of Daisy had not been as straightforward as it might have been. There had been certain mysterious arrangements to be made, hints of dark secrets.

'You got to wait while I get fings ready,' she told her parents, once the purchase of the goat had been made. 'I got to go in the garden and I got to go up to Grandma's room and I got some fings to do yet. Come on, Billy Goat Gruff!'

She went out into the garden with a submissive Billy Goat Gruff in tow. It was hard at that moment for any-body but Mrs Fosdyke and Mr Bagthorpe to believe that his nature was anything but soft to the point of soppiness.

The latter, realizing this, said:

'If she's not back in five minutes, you'd better send out a search-party, Russell. Even man-eating tigers stop for a breather sometimes.'

This remark was made partly to justify his own earlier tirade about the animal's behaviour, and partly with the intention of sending Aunt Celia into a full-scale flap. It failed signally on both counts.

'We are all aware, Henry, that you have no affinity whatever with animals,' Grandma told him coldly, 'unlike Daisy, who is a child of nature.'

'Even the birds of the forest would fly to her bidding,' cooed Aunt Celia, making her daughter sound like St Francis of Assisi, to whom, the rest well knew, Daisy bore not even a passing resemblance.

A fairly heated debate about Daisy's character then began, interrupted only by the return of its subject, beaming happily.

'Everyfing's all right,' she announced contentedly.

They all assumed, mistakenly as it turned out, that she had been making a final tour of Highgate Cemetery, or paying her last respects to Arry Awk.

'Now I got to go up to Grandma Bag's room,' she told them. 'Come on, Billy Goat Gruff!'

'But really, Daisy dear,' protested Mrs Bagthorpe weakly, 'I really do not think that the goat should be taken upstairs.'

'You see, Russell?' said Mr Bagthorpe delightedly. 'You see now what you'll be sharing hearth and home with for the next God knows how many years? It is a young animal, and I have read somewhere, I think, that the life expectancy of a goat is somewhere in the region of forty years. It will see you all into your graves, and sooner rather than later, I should guess.'

'Unless, of course, it gets run over in the drive,' William said.

Uncle Parker was well and truly caught in the crossfire. It was wonderful how the Bagthorpes so often managed to manipulate their own disasters to encompass other people. Uncle Parker kept up his cool front, but was very unhappy. He had forked out seventy pounds for a goat for whom, on sight, he had felt instant distaste, and it now did indeed appear that this animal was to be as inseparable from Daisy as Arry Awk had been. This would make life uncomfortable, almost certainly smelly, and possibly even more expensive than it had been during Arry Awk's regime.

Mr Bagthorpe's good humour, on the other hand, was increasing by the moment. He had rid himself of the goat at a handsome profit, secured Daisy's simultaneous departure and was definitely one up on his old adversary. Characteristically, he could not resist rubbing salt in the wound.

'Let the child take the animal upstairs,' he told his wife. 'Let's find out if it's house-trained, eh, Russell?'

Daisy and the goat trotted out, followed by Grandma. Those in the kitchen could hear scuffling as the goat's hoofs slid on the rugs on the polished floor in the hall. 'It's to be 'oped it's not scratching up my parquet,' Mrs Fosdyke said to Mrs Bagthorpe, almost threateningly.

'It is indeed, Mrs Fosdyke,' said Mr Bagthorpe, forestalling his wife's reply and making this one of the rare occasions when he actually entered into any kind of direct conversation with Mrs Fosdyke. 'Fair acreage of parquet yourself, haven't you, Russell?'

'Though not 'im that 'as to polish it, I daresay,' said Mrs Fosdyke sourly.

'Indeed no! There you have a point!' Mr Bagthorpe exclaimed, seizing the opportunity to inflame matters further. 'Will your own housekeeper be inclined to take to the animal, Russell? Or up and leave, d'you think? There can hardly be any small print in her contract relating to a goat – house-trained or otherwise.'

'Oh dear,' said Aunt Celia faintly.

Mr Bagthorpe, satisfied, sank back into his chair. The best way to get to Uncle Parker was through Aunt Celia, who was less equipped to do her own housework than most ladies. Her fingers were long and white and tapering – though they did sometimes arrange flowers. At The

Knoll, household duties of a more mundane nature were performed by a personage called Mrs Bend, who lived not in Passingham, but a nearby village. She came in every day on a bicycle, come hell or high water, which would seem to indicate that she was made of fairly strong stuff – as, indeed, she needed to be. What with Daisy's writing on walls and setting fire to things in corners and experimenting with water, life at The Knoll, as often as not, *was* hell and high water.

It could not, Mr Bagthorpe further reflected, be easy for this Mrs Bend to get on to Celia's wavelength. Nobody found it easy – or possible, even. Housekeepers generally like their employers to be recognizably of this world, and Mr Bagthorpe knew that Mrs Fosdyke, for instance, would not long tolerate an employer who was always gliding about with her eyes glazed, throwing pots or lying in a darkened room. That Mrs Bend did tolerate all this was a further indication that she was a lady who was not easily thrown.

Most people, on the other hand, have a breaking point. Mrs Bend's, he gleefully told himself, could well turn out to be the goat. He found himself speaking his thoughts out loud.

'They'll chew anything, of course, goats. They say they can go for months without food, as such. They'll manage on things like rugs and upholstery and curtains, and such. Water, that's the only thing you need give 'em.'

'You're overdoing it, Father,' William said. 'We get the message.'

He was afraid that if his father needled Uncle Parker beyond endurance, the Banquet could yet be cancelled.

At this point Daisy and the goat reappeared, followed by Grandma, the latter looking pleased.

'The animal is *not* house-trained,' she informed the company. 'We discovered this on the landing.'

Had the discovery been made in her own room she

173

would, presumably, have looked less pleased. Mrs Fosdyke let out an exclamation of disgust. There was nothing in the small print of *her* contract, either, about goats.

'I'll be off now, Mrs Bagthorpe,' she said, whipping off her overall. 'Dental appointment, you'll remember'–scooting over towards her coat at a rate fast even by her own standards. The door had banged behind her within the minute.

'I said goodbye to Little Tommy,' Daisy said, 'and Grandma gave me this pretty box to put fings in.'

'Lovely, darling!' cooed Aunt Celia.

'It is not to be a parting present,' Grandma told her. 'Darling Daisy and I shall keep in close touch. I have promised to report to her daily on the progress of the kitten, and have also undertaken to come over from time to time and assist her with the training of the goat.'

'Good idea, Mother!' exclaimed Mr Bagthorpe heartily.

Grandma's influence on the goat could not be anything but bad. The goat's behaviour would spiral downwards at the speed of light.

At this moment the telephone rang and Jack went to answer it. He quickly reappeared.

'For you,' he told his mother. 'Hospital.'

Everyone's worst fears were confirmed on Mrs Bagthorpe's return a minute later.

'Great Aunt Lucy is to be discharged tomorrow,' she told everyone. 'The sister says she is much rested, and quite ready to go home.'

'Then they'd better put her in an ambulance and *send* her home,' said Mr Bagthorpe, his mood undergoing an abrupt change at this reminder of his own problems. 'She need not imagine that *I* am driving all the way to Torquay.'

'But – when I say *home*, dear, I mean *here*,' Mrs Bagthorpe faltered. She had meant to prepare her husband for this eventuality, but had never quite seemed to find the right moment to do so. 'She will require some attention for a while to come.'

'Look, Laura,' said her husband, 'the last place anybody can look for any attention of any kind is in this godforsaken household. And at the moment, some of us are still sane. A few more days of kippers at the full moon and buttered scones at dawn, and we shall *all* require hospitalization.'

'But, Henry dear, I told you. Lucy now believes in Time. She believes in it *implicitly*.'

'So you say,' he returned. 'Even if it is true, this news is of no comfort to me whatever. Nobody round here *knows* Lucy like I know her. People with Bees buzzing around in their Bonnets like her don't change their spots overnight. If, as you maintain, she *does* believe in Time, she will not be believing in it like any common or garden mortal. She will have spun round a full one hundred and eighty degrees, like any damn politician.'

'Which is to say?' Mrs Bagthorpe was now rather cool. Every now and again she found her husband's exaggerations intensely trying.

'Which is to say,' continued Mr Bagthorpe, 'that she will now be working to the clock like any bolshy trade unionist. She will have armed herself with a stop-watch. She will have carved the day up into segments. She will want everthing done spot on, to the nearest fraction of a second. We shall all be regimented out of our minds. She will probably insist on bells being rung, like in the navy. You'll see.'

There was a pause.

'The Sister did say something about...' Mrs Bagthorpe's voice trailed off.

'About *what*, Laura?' Mr Bagthorpe demanded.

'Oh dear – about being sure to pick her up at eleven o'clock *sharp* ...'

Mr Bagthorpe groaned.

Chapter Sixteen

Mr Bagthorpe's prophecies about Great Aunt Lucy turned out to be almost accurate.

Nearly everybody heard, with misgivings, her first words on arrival at Unicorn House. The hall clock was just striking noon. She held up a hand, forestalling Mrs Bagthorpe's effusive welcome.

'Ah!' she exclaimed. 'The stroke of twelve!'

She heard the chimes out, and made everyone else do the same, before saying with satisfaction, 'There is something so *rounded* about the stroke of twelve, I always feel. Don't you?'

Nobody knew what to say to this, except Grandma.

'I find it a quite undistinguished hour,' she said. 'So far as I am concerned, one hour is much the same as another. Are you sure you are quite recovered, Lucy? You are still pale – though that may be, of course, the shade of your powder.'

Great Aunt Lucy did not hear any of this because she was fishing, with the hand that was not holding her stick, into her pocket.

'Ah!' She drew out a large and ancient timepiece. This she consulted, and instantly exclaimed:

'But the clock is wrong! There are still two minutes before twelve!'

'You are mistaken, Lucy,' said Grandma calmly. 'That clock was a wedding present from myself to Henry and Laura and keeps perfect time. It has never lost a minute in eighteen years.'

'But my own timepiece is accurate to within fractions of a second!' Great Aunt Lucy was already becoming agitated, the Bees were buzzing ominously. 'I have had it overhauled by a master clockmaker. Quickly, turn on the wireless! We must check!'

'Jack, switch on the portable in the kitchen,' his mother told him.

'I can't,' he said. 'All the radios are in the garden, remember, playing Radio Three to Tess's seeds.'

He knew this for a fact. He would not part with his own transistor from Mondays to Fridays until he had heard Terry Wogan. When he had taken it out that morning, just after ten, the vegetable garden had already been in full concert, with radios and tape recorders everywhere. He remembered glancing over to the meadow beyond, with its giant oak and beech trees, and wondering how they had got to be that size without the benefit of music? He had actually voiced his thought to Tess, who had said witheringly:

'Yes, and look how long it's taken them! Centuries! My own seedlings are already through, within the week.'

Jack thought the analogy between radishes and oaks an unfair one, but did not say so. He rarely entered into argument with any of his siblings, because they were so much cleverer than he.

At this point Mr Bagthorpe, surprisingly, ordered, 'You go and get that transistor and put it back where it belongs. This benighted country could be overrun by Martians, and we'd never know, for all the news we ever get to hear these days.'

Jack went. His father really was very difficult to understand. Mr Bagthorpe hardly ever listened to or read the news. He did not care for it, he said. Even Jack could see that he got politicians hopelessly mixed up and was always confusing Presidents of different countries, and even the countries themselves.

Jack would not have been so surprised by his father's apparent change of heart had he been present in the car during the drive back from hospital. Great Aunt Lucy had been so genuinely effusive in her thanks to Mr Bagthorpe for restoring her belief in Time that he had been impressed despite himself.

'Just think, Henry, if you had not placed that bag of mushrooms for me to trip over, none of this would ever have happened!'

'That's true, I suppose,' he agreed.

'And I shall be eternally grateful, Henry,' she continued. 'I shall never forget who was the instrument of my newfound happiness.'

All this sounded very promising. Mr Bagthorpe had every reason to be wary of any apparent changes of heart in this particular relative, but she had, he reflected, already been converted to Time for nearly three weeks. This phase was apparently ticking over very nicely. And given her obvious gratitude to himself, it now seemed that he could again be in with a chance in the inheritance stakes. It would do no harm, he decided, to humour her for the remainder of her stay.

None the less, he was to find this as trying as did the rest of the family. His aunt's conversation was tedious to a degree, being confined almost entirely to time checks, and there were frequent altercations with Grandma, whose own sense of Time now seemed to have slipped badly. She was late for every meal, and on one occasion almost succeeded in destroying at a single blow Aunt Lucy's newly discovered confidence in Time. She telephoned the Speaking Clock, with the wireless beside her giving a time check, and triumphantly reported that either the BBC or the GPO was three seconds out.

Whether or not this was true nobody knew. The immediate outcome was that Great Aunt Lucy herself took to telephoning the Speaking Clock on the hour, with the wireless beside her. Every now and then she would ring *between* hours, to catch it off guard, as it were. Mr Bagthorpe was enraged by this practice, and laid the blame for it squarely at Grandma's door.

'When the telephone bill arrives,' he told her, 'you will foot it. And you may even find yourself paying for my having a nervous breakdown. It now feels to me as if there are many more than twenty-four hours in a day. My whole body and brain rhythms have been overturned. I am suffering from chronic jet lag.'

The rest of the Bagthorpes were irritated by Great Aunt Lucy, but not beyond endurance. They comforted themselves with the prospect of the Parker Banquet on the horizon, this to be followed by the departure of their guest to Torquay (where she would doubtless embark on the life-long work of having all her haywire timepieces thoroughly overhauled and tested).

Tess was the sole member of the family really interested in Great Aunt Lucy's revised world view. The only trouble was, she was constantly trying to make the old lady revert to her former stance.

'There is no such thing as Time,' she insisted. A lot of the books she was currently reading advanced this theory. Jack sometimes worried about her. The experiments she was making were becoming increasingly bizarre. She had recently, for instance, mounted in a corner of her salad patch an experiment involving cardboard pyramids, razor blades and dead mice. Any razor left under a pyramid shape would sharpen itself automatically, she claimed. The dead mouse under the cardboard pyramid would not decay, she said, whereas the one under an ordinary empty carton certainly would.

'In a week's time I shall remove the coverings and we shall see,' she told everybody. 'The pyramid shape has extraordinary powers, as the ancient Egyptians were well aware.'

'So if we all built outselves pyramid-shaped houses and stopped inside them all our lives, we'd all be immortal, I suppose?' inquired William sarcastically.

'Very probably,' she replied coolly. 'If, of course, there was any such thing as Time.'

There really did seem every danger of Tess exchanging Strings to her Bow for Bees in her Bonnet.

When the day of the Banquet arrived, the younger Bagthorpes, at least, prepared themselves in a state of pleasurable anticipation. They all put on their best things, and Grandma and Great Aunt Lucy were so bejewelled and ornamented in the effort to outdo one another that they would have appeared overdressed even at a Coronation. Mrs Fosdyke had on her best turquoise crimplene and bore two covered baskets containing quantities of stuffed eggs. She was, though she would not have admitted this, pleased at the prospect of overseeing a firm of London caterers, and even allowed Grandpa to sample a couple of eggs in advance. These, judging by his reactions, were well up to standard.

The first hint of a cloud on the horizon came when Grandma requested Jack to go up to her room and fetch the cat basket.

'Cat basket?' repeated Mr Bagthorpe sharply, overhearing this. 'Why in the devil's name do we require a cat basket?'

'Because there is no question of a Banquet without the presence of Thomas the Second,' she replied. (She had ceased to refer to the kitten as Little Tommy immediately after his change in ownership, understandably feeling that this title did not command respect.)

'If that cat goes,' her son told her, 'then I don't.'

'That is entirely up to you, Henry,' she told him calmly. 'He received a specific invitation this morning from Daisy herself. As this Banquet is in her honour, I would not dream of disappointing her.'

Mrs Bagthorpe here smoothly interposed in an effort to extract her husband from a seeming impasse without loss of face.

'Do hurry up and fetch the basket, Jack. It shall travel in my car. Father, Mother, Jack and Rosie – you will travel with myself.'

At this Mr Bagthorpe stamped out muttering, followed by his own allocation of passengers, and the confrontation was thus resolved. Jack himself could not help feeling that the respite was only temporary. Judging by the hissings and scratchings from inside the basket he went to fetch, Thomas the Second had been trained up with great effectiveness. Also, he alone, besides Great Aunt Lucy, knew that a similar basket, containing the formidable Wung Foo, was already reposing on the back seat of Mr Bagthorpe's car. He had been given a pound note for putting it there.

When the Bagthorpes arrived at The Knoll they saw at a glance that the Banquet was going to be a thoroughgoing affair. Already parked in front of the house were two vans and a Rolls Royce, which turned out to be the property of the head chef. Mr Bagthorpe did not at the time know this, and leapt to the conclusion that the Rolls was a recent acquisition of Uncle Parker's, left in this prominent position with the express intention of impressing and infuriating himself. He did not fail to respond.

'My God!' he exclaimed in disgust, climbing out of his own battered estate. 'Look at that, will you! A parasite on society and – if ever there is a bloody revolution in this country, it will be that gin-swigging tailor's dummy and his likes that bring it on. He spends his entire life . . .'

On he raved, giving Jack the opportunity to carry Wung Foo's basket into The Knoll unobserved. Daisy was already hopping up and down at the door. She was got up in what looked to Jack like a Miss Muffet fancy-

dress costume, and was leading Billy Goat Gruff by a
matching silk ribbon with a large bow at the neck.

'Zack, Zack!' she squealed. 'Ooooh, it's going to be –'

'Later, Daisy,' Jack told her. 'You look smashing.
Where can I hide this?'

Daisy, who was a born conspirator or nothing, pointed
to a panelled door, and Jack swiftly opened it and depo-
sited the basket with relief. He had only an instant to
register that the room seemed to be somebody's study,
and thought how fortunate it was that it was not his
father's.

Aunt Celia and Uncle Parker were now approaching,
the former attired in a dress that, even to Jack's uninterested eye, was clearly a replica of Daisy's – or vice versa, of course. Uncle Parker, he noted, looked more or less
as usual, in a pale-green suit with matching waistcoat.

'Hello, there!' he greeted Jack. 'And by Jove, Grandma, what a get up! Welcome to The Knoll. And to yourself, Lucy. How are you?'

He was sufficiently tactful not to comment on Great Aunt Lucy's attire, too, but Jack was already beginning to feel uneasily that the whole set-up had a nursery tale feel of unreality, what with Aunt Celia and Daisy got up as Miss Muffet or Little Bo Peep, and the two elder ladies looking as if, as well as rings on their fingers, they might well have bells on their toes.

Mr Bagthorpe, still under the misapprehension that Uncle Parker was the owner of a brand new Rolls, brushed straight past him and demanded of his sister:

'Where shall I put this accursed cat?'

'I'll take it, Father,' said Jack swiftly and with what at the time he imagined to be great cunning. He took the basket from his father's grasp and, quickly opening and shutting the same door as before, gave a sigh of relief.

'That's them out of the way,' he thought.

Such was the babble and general air of hospitality and goodwill in the hall, that one would have imagined Aunt Celia to have been nominated hostess of the season. She seemed quite to have forgotten her dread of intrusive vibrations in general and those of the Bagthorpes in particular. If anything, Jack thought, she was overdoing it. There was certainly no need to embrace Mr Bagthorpe, and it was clear from the latter's expression that he thought the same.

As few people were acquainted with the layout of The Knoll after so many years of absence, they all hung around in the hall waiting to be shown elsewhere.

'Shall I be getting along to the kitchen?' inquired Mrs Fosdyke loudly at length. 'If you'll be so good as to show me where?'

'Ah, Mrs Fosdyke!' Uncle Parker bowed gallantly. 'I

shall myself take your incomparable stuffed eggs through, and you, I hope, will join us in the drawing-room for champagne.'

They all found themselves in a large room with French windows opening on to the garden and one burnt-out corner. Jack, once in, nipped out again, intending to accost Uncle Parker on his return from the kitchen and apprise him of the presence of Wung Foo and Thomas the Second. Uncle Parker, however, returned at speed, and clearly had his own problems.

'Got to keep Fozzy out of there, if we can,' he whispered loudly in passing. 'Old Bend's just about had enough as it is, with that damn goat. I'll get cracking with the champagne.'

This he duly did, with a vengeance, though the younger Bagthorpes were impatient of what seemed to them an unnecessary postponement of the real business – the Banquet.

'The present, Daddy, the present!' Jack heard Daisy squeal above the general hubbub.

He did not much like the sound of this. Surely Uncle Parker had not already commissioned a replica of the replica of the original replica of Thomas the First? He hoped not, if only because this would certainly remind Grandma of the live Thomas, and this in turn would remind Great Aunt Lucy of Wung Foo, and there might be some gruesome snowballing of events that would finish the Banquet before it even got started, and leave half the company in need of tetanus shots.

As it happened, Grandma was not to be the recipient. Uncle Parker, after first calling for silence (and obtaining it only with difficulty) made a short speech.

'We are all aware,' he began, 'that this Banquet is in honour of Daisy.'

'An' Billy Goat Gruff!' squealed that infant.

'Precisely,' he nodded. 'But it is also, we feel, fitting

184

that we celebrate the recovery of dear Aunt Lucy, and her first visit to our home.'

He here bowed to that lady, and both Grandma and Mr Bagthorpe assumed expressions of extreme displeasure. The former, of course, was jealous. The latter was already beginning to scent a plot laid by the Parkers with the intent of attracting a sizeable slice of Great Aunt Lucy's fortune in their direction.

'Celia and I have learned of your conversion to Time,' he went on, 'and rejoice in it. We congratulate you upon it. We were therefore determined that you should not leave without what is the oldest and most accurate time-piece known to man. If every clock in the world stopped tomorrow, if the BBC blew up and the GPO got its lines tangled for once and all, you, dear, Aunt Lucy, would nevertheless be not a whit worst off.'

'As long as the sun shines, dearest,' murmured Aunt Celia, but nobody really heard this because Uncle Parker now, with a sweeping movement, removed a drape from an object that had been standing unnoticed by the French doors. It was a stone sundial.

Instant silence fell. All the Bagthorpes knew a master stroke when they saw one.

In the end Great Aunt Lucy herself advanced slowly, like a somnambulist.

'Time by the sun is yours for ever, Lucy,' Uncle Parker told her.

'By the sun, and by the moon!' she exclaimed in awe-struck tones.

'And by the moon,' affirmed Uncle Parker. Jack had not thought of this. Could a sundial be also a moondial, he wondered? He noticed that his father's hands were clenching and unclenching ominously, and that Grandma was already drawing herself up in the way she did when about to pronounce.

Uncle Parker had also evidently sensed that the

occasion would rapidly deteriorate, and was prepared for this.

'And now – the Banquet!' he announced. He strode forward, pulled at a rope, and a pair of green velvet curtains swept back to reveal what looked at first sight like a jungle.

'I have garlanded the banquet hall with flowers!' cried Aunt Celia ecstatically – and unnecessarily.

She certainly had. The scene now before them would have left the Tropical House at Kew, as Mr Bagthorpe later observed, standing. Especially as this well-known place does not have boars with apples in their mouths poking out of the greenery and mounds of pineapples, or a string quartet.

At a signal from Uncle Parker – carefully timed to fall between the gasp of astonishment from the assembly and the hubbub that would inevitably ensue if given the chance – a gay Mozart air struck up from somewhere among a clump of potted palms in the far corner of the room. This, it later turned out, had been the inspiration of Aunt Celia, who, having once embarked on playing the role of hostess, had evidently been taken over by it hook, line and sinker.

The Bagthorpes advanced, boggling. The board before them was groaning beyond even their wildest dreams, and was the more exotic for seeming to be sited in a tropical rain forest. Had cockatoos been perched on the chandeliers they would scarcely have seemed inappropriate. Mrs Fosdyke, herself a caterer of no mean order, boggled more than anyone. She was unprepared not only for the overwhelming greenery aspect of things, but also for the presence of at least six waiters in tie and tails standing stiffly to attention.

'For all the world like a set of stuffed penguins in a jungle,' she later told her friends, with a fine disregard for geography. 'And four more of 'em fiddling and blowing in the corner like mad things. She's mad, that Mrs Parker, and haven't I always said so?'

At the time, however, she was too dazed and dosed with champagne to do more than take a seat at the place Uncle Parker had cunningly had laid for her. He thought it safer to have her in sight as a guest than out of sight sabotaging activities in the kitchen. He diplomatically signalled to a waiter bearing a large silver platter of Mrs Fosdyke's stuffed eggs, garnished lavishly with parsley. This was placed, with an expression of outstanding disdain on the face of its server, in a central position on the table.

The five other waiters then closed in, and the Banquet was under way. It began surprisingly well. The long-starved Bagthorpes fell upon the food with a will. Conversation was thin on the ground and there was virtually no lively interchange of views and opinions. A neutral observer would have formed the impression that the guests had been given five minutes in which to consume enough nutriment to last them for the next calendar month. The waiters themselves formed more or less this opinion, and as the meal progressed their lips curled the more. They were accustomed to the kind of people who pick at things, and push away their plates half empty. No plate was likely to be left half empty at this gathering.

Unfortunately, Daisy herself was not hungry. She had had unlimited access to Grandma's Fortnum and Mason hamper during her stay at Unicorn House, and had fed well since her return. She began to find the spectacle of so many people stuffing themselves and paying no attention to herself and Billy Goat Gruff, depressing. Her eye fell speculatively on the small covered tureen by her plate. She shook her head sadly.

'You got to stay on, lid,' she told it.

She cast around for something that would cheer her up, and almost at once remembered the two baskets she had seen Jack deposit in her father's study. Despite her seemingly careless reassignment of Little Tommy to Grandma, Daisy had become genuinely fond of him. It seemed a pity for him to miss the proceedings. She wound her goat's ribbon loosely around the back of her chair and trotted out, unnoticed by anybody.

Now Daisy had intended only to introduce the kitten into the party. She had no real reason to feel affection for Wung Foo, and indeed still bore the marks of his bite. She said later that it had been the sad little whimpering noises from his basket that had upset her.

For whatever reason, then, once she had loosed Little Tommy and given him a good cuddle, she turned her attention to the other basket.

'I better not mix them,' she thought wisely. 'I'll put Little Tommy in the party, then I'll come and fetch the Pekey on his lead and take him to the old griffin.'

She accordingly went back to the hall and, half opening the dining-room door, slipped Tommy through. She then returned and opened Wung Foo's basket. By the time she saw her mistake it was too late. The Pekingese was out at a bound and through the door. Daisy gave chase, but Wung Foo was not even wearing a lead at which she could clutch.

'Oh dear!' she squealed – and lost her head.

The Bagthorpes never really knew what hit them. One minute they all had their heads down, feeding deliriously, the next the table was rocking, pots breaking on all sides and a jungle coming down about their ears. The people who did most yelling (and competition was keen) were the London caterers, who had not been conditioned to this kind of scene. Two of them witnessed the dislodging of the lid of Daisy's tureen, and saw the mass of writhing white maggots which had certainly been no part of the set menu. They became quite hysterical and ran straight out of the house, although not before one of them had been bitten by Wung Foo.

The goat, who had recently been kept on a fairly tight rein by his possessive owner, was now hell-bent on a field day. He reverted to form. Only Mr Bagthorpe had reason to be pleased about this. At least now the rest of his family had seen the animal in its killing mood. It charged indiscriminately at everything. If there had been a troll present, it would have charged at that.

Jack tore at the streamers of vine and ivy tangled about his head and looked wildly about for the three loose animals. This was not easy, because they were all moving very fast. By now, everybody was moving very fast.

When Mr Bagthorpe yelled, 'Out – all of you! Get the hell out of here!' Jack, for one, was inclined to obey. So, it seemed, was everybody else. The younger Bagthorpes made for the door after their father, leaving their mother to help Grandpa with Grandma, who was shrieking, 'Get him, Thomas, get him!' and carried on shrieking this even as she was bundled into the car.

As the cars simultaneously revved up Uncle Parker lurched out of the front door, a garland of roses and ivy draped over his right ear. He was yelling something, but nobody waited to hear what.

'Thank God we're out of that!' Mr Bagthorpe exclaimed fervently as he threw the car out of the drive in the direction of home.

Epilogue

Mr Bagthorpe's thankfulness was short-lived, as it turned out, because when they arrived home it was to find that most of the wine which he had finally succeeded in making had blown up in their absence. Some of it, indeed, was still in the process of blowing up. The floor, ceiling and walls of the kitchen were spattered with red and yellow juices, and broken glass was strewn everywhere. It was at this stage that the Bagthorpes realized that in their haste to retreat they had forgotten Mrs Fosdyke – last seen spread-eagled in a pile of her own stuffed eggs. (They had also forgotten Great Aunt Lucy, but did not notice this until later).

Nobody dared enter the kitchen, because a wine jar blew up just as they were opening the door. Mrs Bagthorpe was quite distraught.

'How shall we ever use the kitchen again?' she cried. 'We dare not touch the bottles! They are as volatile as gelignite!'

'Henry must move them,' said Grandma. 'He would not heed a mother's warning, and must pay the price.'

'Or get the Explosives and Anti-bomb Squad in,' William suggested.

Mr Bagthorpe was by and large in favour of this, even though the suggestion had been made in a spirit of sarcasm. He was unwilling, however, to risk the attendant publicity. What they did in the end, then, was defuse the remaining bottles themselves. They did this by crouching behind the kitchen door and hurling bricks and stones at the jars and bottles. None of them was very good at aiming, and a good deal of Mrs Bagthorpe's blue Staffordshire pottery ended up in pieces. Mr Bagthorpe's wine, per bottle, had cost rather more than vintage champagne, William later worked out.

The exploding of the wine- and, as it later transpired, beer-bottles certainly sounded the knell of Self-Sufficiency. Even Mr Bagthorpe could now see that it would be cheaper to revert to being un-Self-Sufficient.

Once the bottles had been defused the Bagthorpes gingerly advanced into their shattered kitchen just as the telephone rang. Jack picked his way through the debris and answered it. The voice on the other end of the line was unmistakable. Jack listened numbly to the text-strewn effusion that followed. When at last the voice stopped, 'Jolly good,' Jack croaked, 'I'll tell the others'– and hung up. Luke had become Young Brain of Britain.

He did not, of course, tell the others. By tomorrow morning they would know anyway. They would read it in the newspaper. He returned to the kitchen.

'Wrong number,' he said, but nobody was listening.

'Let your grandmother in through the front door, Jack,' his mother told him. 'She cannot be expected to go through all this. She must need to rest.'

She did not, of course. Adrenalin was coursing through her veins as furiously as through anyone else's. At this point Tess, who had gone running straight off into the darkening garden once she had hurled her share of bricks, returned in a state of near-hysteria. She too had caught a glimpse of Daisy's tureen of maggots and had put two and two together. Daisy had dislodged her dead mouse experiment.

'I'll kill her!' she screamed.

Nobody attempted to dissuade her from this course of action, even Grandma, who had by now realized that Thomas, as well as Mrs Fosdyke and Great Aunt Lucy, had been abandoned at The Knoll. She was evidently not sufficiently confident of the effects of her intensive training to be sure that he had killed or severely maimed the other two animals at large, and her pride would not allow her to telephone and find out. (It later emerged that the only casualties had been human ones.)

When the dust finally settled all that had really happened was that the Bagthorpes returned to normal – or as normal as they would ever be. Self-Sufficiency was abandoned, hopes of a legacy from Great Aunt Lucy relinquished, and Mrs Fosdyke finally persuaded to return, once the kitchen had been redecorated. Mr Bagthorpe and Uncle Parker each had sufficient ammunition to last them in their rows for months, if they spaced it out properly.

Jack himself was pleased with the long-term outcome of the final débacle. Of all the pets owned by the family, Zero alone had been absent and free from all blame. He had been guarding Jack's comics up in his room, even through all the exploding going on below. Even Mr Bagthorpe conceded his innocence.

'Numskulled and mutton-headed that hound may be,' he said, 'but at least he's not a killer'– which was the nearest he would ever come to paying Zero a compliment.